WARRENDALE

Athena Morningstar Kelly

ISBN: 0963702912
ISBN-13: 9780963702913

DEDICATION

To the Good Ole Neighborhood 48227 and 48228
and to my brother, Luke; Gwen, David and Kenny.
RIP

ACKNOWLEDGMENTS

With great appreciation to my technical advisor and buddy, Jimmy Soules, who went from the mean streets of the Rebels and the 48227 to a badge.

.

PROLOGUE TO
CHAPTER ONE

I was grocery shopping at Meijer with my 15 year old grandson, Jake, and I said, "Well, I'll be dammed." (I don't even remember why I said it.)

"Yes, you will," he replied.

"Hey, that's not nice to say to your Granny," I laughed.

"You said it."

"You're right, I did."

"I don't even know what that means."

"Neither do I."

Now, I've been trying to write this book for 4 years and I get caught up in every little fact because I want to be accurate. Do I write it in the first person "me" or recount it like the sometimes tragic, sometimes shocking story I was a part of? Do I recount everything? There are some things so bad I just don't think I should tell. And the dates, even though I have been writing details and memories down for at least 39 years, I wasn't sure what year Boone, Ray and Van died so I had to call Taylor because she knows everything. She's my go to person.

"What year did Van and Boone die? Was it 1979 or 1980? Michael was born in 1979 so I think it was 1980."

"After all these years, why in the hell do you care?"

"Because I'm trying to remember and I can't and it's making me crazy." I knew that would hook her because if she can't remember something it makes her a little nuts until she does and I couldn't tell her the truth because I'm writing a book about what happened to her and Van and what happened to the rest of us that were along for the crazy ass ride.

"I'm pretty sure they died in 1981."

"What about Ray?"

"I don't know and I don't care."

"Can you please look it up on Ancestry.com and let me know?"

"I think you're nuts but I'll do it anyway. I'll e-mail it to you but quit thinking about all this shit, it doesn't do any good. Leave it in the past where it belongs. I forgave Van years ago but I still don't want to think about it."

I shoved a whole Pepperidge Farm Milano cookie into my mouth so I couldn't talk; made a muffled noise agreeing with her and hung up the phone relieved I didn't crack and tell her what I was really doing.

I hope I won't be damned for telling this story that should remain in the past. Like the Naked City, there are many stories in Warrendale and this is one of them.

CHAPTER ONE

NOVEMBER, 1981

They found him sitting alone in the woods next to the rented house he lived in with his second wife and her two daughters, his back against the tree with his left shoulder blown off. The rifle was lying on the ground next to his right hand, its barrel pointing away from his body. His eyes were wide open, his mouth was shut. He was dead.

Ken Kowalski drove 80 miles to hunt with his buddy on opening day but instead of tracking deer, he was sitting in his truck on the dirt road, listening to the radio, smoking a cigarette and watching two guys walking out of the woods carrying a body on a stretcher covered up with a sheet. The Detroit cops would have asked him why he was sitting there but the one small town cop walking behind the stretcher didn't seem to care. He didn't know who was on the stretcher but he had a damn good idea then an arm fell out and there was the red rose tattoo with the black inked in ribbon and he knew immediately. He took a long drag off of his cigarette, put the truck in gear and headed back to Detroit. After he got back home, he waited a few hours before he went up to the Warrendale Bar to hang out with the guys. When they asked why he was back so soon, he lied and said he never left.

It would be decades before he told anybody he was there and when he finally did tell someone, it was Taylor Ginetti Thomas.

Other than examining the rifle found next to Van's body, there was no investigation, not even an autopsy. The funeral director ruled he bled to death as a result of a self-inflicted gunshot wound but not everybody believed it and his death was the topic of conversation for a long, long time. Maybe he didn't have the safety on; he tripped and his rifle went off; it might have been a drug deal gone bad; maybe Mark Poole's family finally got their revenge; or he was depressed over his brother Boone's death, after all he did try to kill himself twice before but who commits suicide by blowing their shoulder off?

So what went wrong? Some thought it was Viet Nam that fucked Van up, others were sure it was his loving mother and the rest thought it was a combination of both.

CHAPTER TWO

VAN AND TAYLOR

Van Robert was born on February 18, 1947 in Detroit, Michigan, the first child of Robert (Bob) and Evelyn Thomas. On August 21, 1948, on the other side of Southfield Road, Taylor Carmen was born, the first child of Giuseppe (Joe) and Carmen Ginetti. Even though they lived a little over a mile away from each other, they met for the first time at Ruddiman Junior High School.

Van and Taylor had completely opposite personalities. Van was outgoing with lots of friends and Taylor was painfully shy and other than hanging around with her next door neighbor, Bee, she pretty much kept to herself. A lot of the guys thought Taylor was stuck up and they didn't get what Van saw in her but he told them she wasn't stuck up, she was just quiet. He liked it that she didn't want or need everybody to be her friend. But they both had one thing in common, they didn't take any shit off of anybody. The difference was Van handled his differences of opinion with his fists and Taylor handled hers with her razor sharp

4

tongue. Then there was Tim Opanowski, Van's best friend, who was an expert at using both.

Van had sky blue eyes and blonde hair that he kept in perfect waterfall. On a scale of 1 to 10, he was a 10 for both good looking and son of a bitch. Wherever he went, whether it was to school or up to Waysides Restaurant, a little hole in the wall hangout on Warren Avenue, he always looked good. He was smart, wild and reckless and all that made him a bad boy chick magnet. Van loved the girls and the girls loved him. Taylor was his first steady girlfriend and he did care about her but that didn't stop him from still hooking up with Maureen Bridges and Jayne Fitzpatrick. He never lied to Maureen and Jayne, they knew about Taylor but the sluts didn't care and, of course, Taylor didn't have a clue.

Taylor stood barely 5 feet tall. She had long jet black hair and brown eyes, genetic markers of her Italian and Spanish heritage. She liked hanging out with Van and Tim. They were a lot of fun. She liked sitting in Ted Cooper's Kitchen and taking to his Mom, Minnie, and Tim's Mom, Cecilia, but she really liked going over to Van's house because it was exciting there with six kids and the chaos of their every day life. Just like Van enjoyed the calm at Taylor's house; she only had one sister, Lorraine also known as Lor to family and friends, and her parents actually liked each other and didn't fight.

CHAPTER THREE

VAN AND TIM

At 16 years old, Van Thomas and Tim Opanowski were bad ass mother fuckers. They walked down their neighborhood streets like they owned them and because they lived in and belonged to Warrendale, a tough bunch of good looking, cool, be-still-my-heart, Greaser guys, they did. Best friends since Kindergarten, they were together so much that if Tim was alone, the other guys joked that Van was somewhere knocking off a piece of ass but only Tim knew for sure if he was. Tim kept Van's secrets and watched his back. If Taylor or Van's Mom were looking for him, Tim always knew where to find Van and then, and only then, would he go get him.

Warrendale was a predominately white, Polish Catholic middle class, blue collar neighborhood on the northwest side of Detroit ending at Paul Street, one step the other side of Paul into Ford Woods and you were in Dearborn. The houses were mostly modest two bedroom asbestos-sided bungalows with finished basements and converted attics, mixed in with the occasional single story wood frame house or a big old house in the shape of a barn. The homes were clean, the yards were immaculate with flowers and vegetable gardens and the only area code was 313. It looked more like a cozy little town that part of a big city, unless you were a cop at the 14th or 16th Precincts, to them Warrendale was trouble with a capital "T". If a car was stolen, there was a B&E (Breaking and Entering), a guy was stabbed in the back, a store was robbed, or any other kind of assault or crime was committed even if it happened in Grandale, the majority of the time the investigation led the cops to the mean streets of Warrendale.

Warrendale wasn't just the name of their neighborhood; it was the name of their gang. Unlike Grandale whose neighborhood gang was the Rebels, Warrendale bore their neighborhood name with pride. They called each other by their last names or nicknames. They called girls broad, chick, old lady or bitch. If they ran into each other at the store or a restaurant, any place outside of the hood, they'd shout out "KEE AW KEE" just like Jeff and Porky on *Lassie*, punch each other in the arm, bullshit for a minute and be on their way. When some of them decided they wanted tattoos, they dipped a sewing needle into India ink and wrote their names on each others' left bicep; Dave Sullivan inked Matt Dupree, Dupree inked Sullivan, Van inked Tim, Tim inked Van, you get the picture. If you knew them well enough, you could tell by the handwriting who inked who. They shared everything from jail time, probation officers, recruiters, cigarettes, cars, booze and drugs to women. They were bad boys that good girls from bordering neighborhoods couldn't resist. They were juvenile delinquents who in adult life graduated to felon status. They were like *American Graffiti* on acid. They went to dances, raced their cars, hung out at Daly's Drive-In on Greenfield and they cruised Telegraph, but with booze and weapons. As felonious as their collective characters were, even they had standards they lived by: they never dropped a dime on each other and if one of their own got locked up, they chipped in enough money to make bail.

In the end, the only thing that separated them from each other was the Angel of Death.

CHAPTER FOUR

1963
SUMMER

Van got up at 8:00 Saturday morning, jumped down from his top bunk bed and looked at Boone asleep in the bottom bunk and thought how easy is would be to climb back up there, lie down and sleep but he couldn't disappoint the ladies. He'd recently added two more to his harem, Linda, a sales girl at Hudson's in Northland Mall and Mary, a sales girl at Monkey Wards in Wonderland Mall. He stumbled into the bathroom, took his shower and got dressed. He stood in front of the bathroom sink looking at his reflection in the medicine cabinet mirror, brushing his hair into the perfect waterfall. He tucked his pack of camels into the front pocket of his short sleeved black banlon shirt, put his Zippo lighter and switchblade in his front pants pockets and his brush in the back pocket of his tight black continental pants and stepped into his black kicks. He looked good and he knew it; the way he saw it, he wasn't conceited, it was just a fact Jack. He was spraying his waterfall into place when Tim knocked on the screen door.

"Since when do you knock?" Evelyn yelled from the kitchen.

"I'm just being polite," Tim laughed walking in the front door and sitting down in the rocking chair to watch cartoons with Van's sisters, 6 year old Violet and 4 year old twins, Vickie and Valerie. Although between Evelyn's yelling at Bob, and the girls fighting and crying, he was the only one really watching Mighty Mouse save the day. He liked Van's Mom and he'd known her forever. She had a mini stroke after the twins were born, she drank too much and she just wasn't the same. He figured Vita and Boone were still sleeping. That's what he should be doing instead of hopping busses to see broads and not even broads he liked.

Tim's parents separated when he was four years old and he looked forward to seeing his father every other Sunday afternoon for a few hours. Stanislaus and Cecilia Opanowski were strict Polish Catholics and even though they lived in different cities and led different lives, they would never get a divorce because it was wrong in the eyes of God and the Church. Even though Tim had three older sisters and an older brother, there wasn't much fighting at his house, unless Regina wore Natalie's clothes and then his Mom would make him run around the house closing the windows so the neighbors couldn't hear them screaming at each other. Occasionally his Mom would swat him on the ass with her broom to make a point, but she never put much effort into her swing. He couldn't stand it if something ever happened to make her a different person. Even though he probably had the oldest mother in the neighborhood, he loved her just the way she was.

"I'm leaving," Van yelled to his mother hoping she was too involved in bitching out the old man to hear him.

"Wait," Evelyn said running over to Van and smoothing down his collar.

"Stop it, Evelyn," he said pushing her hands off of him. He developed the habit of calling her "Evelyn" instead of

"Mom" to try and piss her off but it didn't work because in her eyes, he could do no wrong.

Van was Evelyn's whole world, a fact she didn't hide from anybody, including her husband or her other kids. What she didn't see was the more attention she paid to him, the further she pushed him away. His Dad was an over-the-road trucker who rolled into town on Friday night and rolled on out again on Sunday afternoon. Van liked the old man well enough because he left him alone.

"You boys be home in time for dinner and be careful." It never occurred to her that it was the other people they came in contact with that had to be careful of them. In her mind, her kids were safe as long as they stayed in Warrendale but she didn't like it when they left the neighborhood.

Van and Tim waited until they were a couple houses down to flip open their Zippos and light their Camels for their three block walk to Warren Avenue to catch the first bus.

"I'm just about done with these fucking bus rides," Tim said.

"What's wrong with you? It's not like you've got anything else to do," Van said.

"Sleep would be nice."

"Quit your bitching, you sound like a little girl. I'll let you sit by the window."

"So I can look at stuff I don't give a shit about. That's big of you. Give me your cigarettes."

"What, fuck no."

"If I have to ride the bus, I want your cigarettes."

"Here, take them," he said throwing the pack of Camels at Tim's head.

"Here's two smokes, see how long they last. Then when you need another smoke and don't have one, you'll know how pissed off I feel about riding the damn bus."

"You're lucky you're my best friend or I'd have to beat you."

"No, you're lucky I'm your best friend because nobody else wants to be. It's not easy being your best friend you know. Evelyn may think you're Mr. Wonderful but I don't."

"Very funny."

"Why was she ragging on your old man?"

"Because she thinks he's got a girlfriend in Kentucky. Last night the old man told me he was sorry he wasn't around more but he had to work and he didn't blame me for running away from home. Can you believe that shit?"

When being Evelyn's favorite child got to be too much for Van to handle, he ran away. Sometimes for a day or two and sometimes for a week or more, with Dave Sullivan or Al Kopka or both. Sometimes they hid out in the rafters of Matt Dupree's garage, a block over on Rutland for Van and Al, and five houses down on the same block for Sullivan. Sometimes in the summer they would hitch a ride 40 miles away to Half Moon Lake. If Al was involved when his Mom got too worried his older brother, Wayne, would find them and make them come home. But Wayne also brought them food and made sure they were okay for as long as they were gone. It was amazing how their parents never knew where they were but half the kids in the neighborhood, including their siblings, were bringing them food.

"Does he?"

"Does he what?"

"Does he have a girlfriend in Kentucky?"

"I hope he does."

"I think she just cares about you too much."

"Ya think? She drives me fucking nuts and this thing she's got about everybody has to be home for dinner. She says with the old man on the road, we need to eat dinner together like a real family. I think she thinks she's Harriet Nelson waiting for Ozzie to come home."

"I guess that makes you David and Boone must be Ricky," Tim laughed.

"What the hell kind of job did Ozzie have anyway? You never saw him go to work. He just walked around wearing a sweater and eating ice cream. I mean, did you ever see Ozzie go to the bar? No, he went to the malt shop."

The busses were running on time and by 1:00PM Van and Tim were standing on Taylor's front porch.

"Hi guys, come on in," Taylor greeted them with a smile.

"Oh look, it's Larry and Moe, where's Curly?" Lorraine asked.

"And I thought the Wicked Witch was dead," Tim countered. "Ding dong."

"If you don't have anything nice to say to each other, don't say anything at all," Carmen said carrying a laundry basket full of clothes up from the basement.

"Sorry, Mrs. G," Tim said.

"Oh, he's sorry when you're here but when you're not he's an ass."

"Lorraine Maria, a lady doesn't talk like that."

Tim and Lor fought like gunfighters that couldn't wait to pull the trigger and didn't want to leave the other one standing, but instead of bullets they used an endless barrage of sarcastic words and insults that cut deeper than the serrated blade on a Ginsu knife.

"Now, what have you boys been up to today?" Carmen asked.

"We watched cartoons with Violet and the twins," Tim answered. "That Mighty Mouse is really something." Other than the "we" part he rationalized he wasn't lying. He had just enough Catholic in him to try to avoid guilt whenever possible.

"Mighty Mouse? I never figured you boys for fans of Mighty Mouse.

"Thanks again for dinner last night," Van said.

Carmen got carryout from Stromboli's every Friday night. She ordered a mushroom and cheese pizza or fish and chips for her family but for Van she always ordered a rib dinner with french fries and cole slaw. Taylor was glad her Mom liked Van but didn't think he should get special treatment because he was lucky enough not to be Catholic and she hated watching him eat those damn ribs.

"We enjoy your company."

"I don't," Lor interjected.

"Lorraine Maria, that's enough.   You kids enjoy yourselves.   There's pop in the fridge and snacks on the kitchen counter.   Come with me missy, we are going to fold clothes."

"Okay, but I'm still going to tell you what I think Tim is." Lorraine followed her mother down the hall, turned around and flipped Tim the bird.

"Your sister is a beast," Tim said.

"You know what your problem is? You can dish it out but you can't take it," Taylor said.

"So what are you saying exactly?"

"What am I saying exactly? Let's see, take it like a man."

"He just doesn't like a girl getting the better of him," Van laughed.

"She'll never get over on me," Tim retorted.

"Oh please, if my mother wasn't home, she would have crucified you and you know it."

Taylor held no illusions that Van was the love of her life or that she was his.   No, Taylor was living in the moment and when it was all over, oh well, she had a good time and life goes on.

After Van and Tim left Taylor's house, they made two more stops; first at Jayne's and then Maureen's house. Maureen lived on the street between theirs', Van one block to the right and Tim to the left.   They had it down to a science, 5 girls in one day and they were home in time for dinner.

SEPTEMBER

Giuseppe Ginetti was finally living the American Dream. He had a good job at the Ford Rouge Plant and came straight home from work every night to have dinner with his wife and kids. He spoke with an Italian accent and that added to his charm. His wife and girls were his whole world. He was bald and short, a little over 5 feet tall. Tim and Van affectionately called him "Big Joe" and the nickname stuck

Giuseppe left Italy when he was 19 years old. His father and sister Sophia were already in America and Sophia's husband, Aldo, a naturalized United States citizen, helped bring him over. His mother and older sister refused to leave Italy and move to America so he tried to visit them every year bringing them perfume, chocolate and nylons, gifts that he knew they would love but wouldn't spend money on for themselves. He'd been living in the U.S. a few months, doing his best to learn the English language and working hard at his job when Aldo told him since he was making a life in America, he should tell people his name was "Joe".

Three years later when his beloved Sophia died in childbirth, he blamed Aldo. Aldo always talked about having many, many babies and as soon as one baby was born, he wanted to have another one. Although Sophia never talked to Joe about it, a blind man could see she was just worn out. He may have been a young man but he was sure four babies in four years killed his delicate sister. He missed her smile and laughing with her. Because he was a strong man, he went through the motions of carrying Sophia's broken body to her grave void of emotion but when he was alone, for a long time he couldn't stop the tears. For the first time in his life he knew what it was like to have a broken heart. While "Joe" stayed on cordial terms with Aldo out of respect, from the day of Sophia's death "Giuseppe" distanced himself as much as he could.

He finally found happiness when he married Carmen and with her came her close knit family. Her parents were born in Spain but Carmen, her brother Carlos and sister Chi Chi were born in the United States. Her father died when she was in her teens so instead of encouraging her daughters to find a man and get married, her mother saw to it that they were well educated. She wanted them to be able to support themselves so that if tragedy struck them as it had her, they could make their way in life.

Carmen was a Registered Nurse in the Emergency Room at Oakwood Hospital. She worked the day shift because she wanted to be home in the evening with her family. In the summer, she rented a tent at Camp Dearborn for two weeks for her and her daughters and Joe, recognizing they enjoyed their "girl time", stayed in the City and spent the weekends with them. He missed Carmen terribly but he knew how important it was to her and he could deny her nothing.

Carmen had dark hair and eyes with beautiful olive-skin that she passed on to her daughters, along with her love of gold jewelry. Her hair and nails were always done. She taught her daughters that appearances were important. "The way people see you is the way people will treat you. You can be the nicest, smartest person in the world but if you don't look good, you won't get a chance to prove it."

On Sundays they went to noon Mass at St. Peter and Paul Catholic Church and they had dinner at Grandma Montes' house with Uncle Carlos, Aunt Chi-Chi and their families.

Every time Joe thought about how happy he was, he got scared. He tried not to think like that but he couldn't stop the sinking feeling in the pit of his stomach that something bad was going to happen. Taylor was born with a hereditary muscle disease. When she was 8 years old, she had surgery on both of her legs to stretch and straighten the muscles. When she was 10, she had surgery on both eyes and as a result, she had to wear glasses with pretty thick lenses. But all the operations were successes, she walked without a limp and she begged them for contact lenses and only wore her glasses at home so even though he tended to think of her as frail, he knew she really wasn't. Lorraine was healthy, Carmen was healthy, he was healthy, and as long as they had their health he knew he could handle anything.

* * *

Carmen wasn't feeling well. She had shooting pains in her back and she was having trouble breathing; she had dark

16

circles under her eyes that were getting increasingly more difficult to cover with make-up. When Joe asked her if she was okay, she told him she thought she caught the flu bug at work. She made an appointment with Dr. Mendoza, their long time family doctor, but she didn't tell Joe because she didn't want him to worry.

Seven days after her she saw Dr. Mendoza and he referred her to Dr. Rayburn, she was diagnosed with stage 3, bordering on stage 4, lung cancer. She put up a brave front for the girls but Joe knew his fear of happiness would no longer be a problem because his wife was going to die and his world was going to end.

MONDAY, NOVEMBER 4TH

Two months after she was diagnosed with cancer and minutes after Taylor left her hospital room, Carmen Montes Ginetti saw the face of God.

There were so many cars in front of Taylor's house, in the driveway and on the street when Taylor and Bee got home, she was afraid to walk inside her house. She stood out front for a couple minutes with Bee and they watched her relatives through the front windows talking and walking from the kitchen, through the dining room, into the living room and back again.

"That's Baptista's car in the driveway," Taylor said.

"You better go inside," Bee said. "I'll call you later."

Taylor had a sick feeling in the pit of her stomach but she finally worked up the courage to walk in her front door.

"Where have you been?" her older half-sister Baptista, Carmen's daughter from her first marriage, screamed. Baptista was eight years old when her father died and she figured that it was just supposed to be her and her mother for the rest of their lives living at Grandma's house. She was so hateful and angry when Carmen married Joe, everybody thought it was best if Baptista continued to live with Grandma Montes. She got angrier when Taylor was born and now she lashed out at Taylor with all the fury she had building up all those years.

"I stopped at Waysides with Bee," Taylor said still not quite sure what was going on.

"You stopped at Waysides with Bee when your mother is dead? What the hell is wrong with you?"

"What are you talking about? Mom's not dead. She can't be dead. I just left her I just left the hospital she wasn't dead. You're lying," Taylor yelled back.

"The nurses tried to catch you but you were already gone," Aunt Chi Chi said taking Taylor's hand in hers.

"No, this can't be. This isn't right," Taylor cried.

"I need mother's pearls for the funeral and I need to go buy a new black dress," Baptista announced.

"Madre Dios, Baptista," Grandma Montes cried out.

Their mother was dead and all Baptista could think about was what to wear to her funeral. Taylor walked past Uncle Carlos and a group of cousins, looked over at Lor and mouthed "that bitch", slammed the door at the bottom of the steps, ran upstairs to her room and cried herself to sleep.

* * *

The next few days were a blur. Taylor was tired of kneeling and smelling incense. She knew there was a rosary at the funeral home and a funeral Mass at St. Peter and Paul. She knew they went to St. Hedwig's Cemetery and watched her mother lowered into a concrete box in the ground. She knew these things happened and a lot of people talked to her, but there were only two things she remembered clearly.

The first thing she remembered was a man her father told her was Uncle Aldo walking in with 10 boys one just a little taller than the other, all dressed alike in navy blue suits with white shirts, blue ties and spit-shined black dress shoes, lining up in front of the casket, kneeling together and making the sign of the cross, praying, getting up together and filing out. She was impressed by how well behaved the boys were and tried to figure out how old they were. She figured that the older ones must be her cousins, her Aunt Sophia's sons.

They knew all about Uncle Aldo and Aunt Sophia because their Dad said he needed to talk about her once in a while because he didn't want her memory to fade away. She wondered if her Dad was afraid that her Mom's memory would fade away. Baptista's sons were only two and three, they wouldn't remember their Grandma. She liked those little guys but Baptista could kiss her ass. Baptista liked Lor and if Lor wanted to be friends with Baptista more power to her. Aunt Chi Chi said Baptista resented Taylor because she was the first one born and that Taylor didn't do anything wrong.

The second thing Taylor clearly remembered was sitting in a chair and watching Baptista standing in front of their Mom's casket in her new black dress and black heels, crying fake tears, twisting their mother's pearls around her index finger and putting on quite a show. She remembered very slowly getting up from the chair, walking up behind Baptista, whispering "fuck you" in her ear and walking out the door.

THURSDAY, NOVEMBER 7TH

They were walking up Paul towards Tim's house and they each took one last long drag off their cigarettes before they ground them out on the sidewalk. They didn't know if Ceclila suspected they smoked but they didn't want to take the chance of finding out if she did. There was a chill in the air and leaves were scattered on the ground. Their matching black leather jackets were never buttoned up no matter how cold it got.

"What's wrong with you? Van asked.

"Nothing," Tim answered. He still couldn't quite wrap his head around what Bee told him.

They were standing on the corner of Longacre and Paul, next to Tim's house.

"Don't bullshit me, I know something's wrong."

"Why didn't you tell me Taylor's Mom died?"

Van shoved Tim so hard that he stumbled backwards and almost fell over. Tim regained his footing, charged at Van, hit him in the stomach and knocked him to the ground.

"Stay down there damn you. Have you lost your mind?"

Van jumped up, grabbed Tim by the throat and put him in a headlock.

"Jesus Christ, cut it out, you're choking me."

"You're lying."

"You dumb fuck," Tim broke Van's hold and they both fell on the ground.

"I'm not going to lie about something like that."

"Who told you she died?"

"Bee, she went to the funeral this morning and wondered why we, especially why you weren't there."

"What did you tell her?"

"I told her I didn't know or I would have been there."

They were too busy rolling around on the ground to notice Ted Cooper walk out of Ford Woods and across Paul, holding his rifle in one hand and swinging two fat, dead squirrels by their tails in the other. He lived in Michigan but he was still a Tennessee boy and he loved squirrel stew. He looked down and gave them each a not to gentle nudge with the toe of his boot. Ted was tall and lanky with a Southern twang and even though he acted easy going, you really didn't want to piss him off.

"What in the hell are you two fighting about? Break it up before Cecilia comes out or worse my Mom comes out."

"He said Taylor's Mom died," Van yelled.

"I know."

"What do you mean you know? How do you know?"

"My Mom told me."

Fuck me, Van thought, more news was broadcast in Minnie's kitchen than on Channel 7. Telephone, telegraph, tell it at Minnie's.

"Why didn't you tell me?"

"You're her boyfriend. Why didn't you tell me asshole? I'd know if Gwen's Mom died."

"So you're the perfect boyfriend.

"Not perfect, just better than you. So are you two done trying to kill each other?"

"Hey, I didn't start this," Tim said pushing Van's hand off of his mouth.

"We're done," Van said helping Tim up.

"I'm going home and if Minnie or Cecilia come out, you boys are on your own," Ted said.

"You're lucky I didn't mess up that pretty face of yours," Van said.

"When's the last time you talked to Taylor?" Tim asked.

"Monday at school."

"Her Mom died on Monday. I should punch you right in the mouth. You're such a fuck. You have to call her," Tim said brushing the leaves off of his clothes.

"I'll call her. I'm going to call her but I don't know what the hell to say. What do I say?"

"Say you're sorry and ask her if she's okay. Ask her how Big Joe and Lor are. I'll call her after you talk to her. I'm glad to hear you finally admit it."

"Admit what?"

"That I have a pretty face."

Tim was good looking but in a different way than Van. At 6 feet he was taller than Van with dark brown almost black hair and brooding brown eyes. This was one of his rare moments of sensitivity and completely out of character. Prone to tactical mood swings, he was more comfortable being a smart ass than a nice guy but that didn't mean his mother hadn't raised him right, it just meant he was selective as to when and where he chose to be kind.

Van frantically smoked another cigarette on the two block walk to his house while he rehearsed what he wanted to say to Taylor. He ran in the house, grabbed the phone out of the dining room, went into the bathroom and closed the door.

"Hey, I need to get in there," Vita said pounding on the bathroom door.

"Cut it out. I got to make a call. I'll be out in a couple minutes." Van dialed the phone and took a deep breath.

"Hello."

"Is Taylor there?"

"This is her Grandma, who is calling?"

"Van Thomas."

"Oh, you are the missing boyfriend?" Grandma Montes barely stood 4 feet 11 inches tall but she was mighty. She was the head of her family and this boy's insult to her granddaughter would not be ignored. She wore glasses with coke bottle lenses but she saw more through those glasses than people with 20/20 vision and she knew no good would come from Taylor's friendship with Van. He was trouble.

"Yes, Maam. I'm sorry I didn't know about Mrs. G., I mean Mrs. Ginetti's passing."

"If you would have called, you would have known my daughter passed away. Am I right young man?"

"Yes, Maam you are and I should have called." Ouch, Van thought. If she was trying to make him feel bad, it was working.

"Taylor, your young man is on the phone."

"DON'T TALK TO HIM," Lorraine screamed.

"Hello," Taylor said.

"I'm sorry about your Mom."

"Okay."

"I didn't know. Bee told Tim this afternoon. We didn't know."

"Okay."

"You should have told me. Why didn't you call me?"

"Gee, my Mom died. I wasn't thinking about calling you. You could have called me. Other people found out and I didn't call them."

"I know and I'm sorry about that, I really am. I screwed up. How are you? How are Big Joe and Lor?"

"I'm fine, we're fine. Thanks for calling."

Click.

He sat cross-legged on the bathroom floor with his back against the bathtub looking at the phone. She didn't even say goodbye. He wanted to throw the phone across the room but if he broke it, he'd be in deep shit. He loved Carmen Ginetti more than Evelyn, how fucked up was that? He should have called Taylor but she should have told him. He didn't know if he was madder at her or himself. It was one wound that would never heal. He would carry his regret to his grave. He said the only prayer he could remember, "Now I lay me down to sleep, I pray the Lord my soul keep. God please keep Mrs. G.'s soul", he whispered, tears welling up in his eyes. This was the worst day of his life.

"Would you get out of there," Vita yelled. One bathroom for eight people sucked she thought..

He opened the door and walked out carrying the phone.

"You're crying."

"If you tell anybody, I'll hurt you and you know I can."

"Geez, I'm not going to tell anybody. My lips are sealed."

Van was four years older than Vita and he'd pushed and shoved her around enough for her to know he meant he'd mess her up and she didn't have a death wish. Boone was two years older than her and he could calm Van down, but Boone wasn't around. Nope, as tempting as it was to work Van over, she wasn't telling anybody that she saw him cry.

* * *

Joe came home from work every night, went to the bedroom he had shared with the love of his life and shut the door. Everything in their room was exactly the way Carmen left it, her clothes were in the closet and dresser drawers and her shoes were under the bed. He couldn't bear to remove their wedding picture, her perfume bottles or jewelry box. He would leave them sitting on top of their dresser until one of the girls said they wanted them. Until that time, they were his private memories of her. He picked up Carmen's pearls. They were the same ones she was wearing in their wedding picture. He took them back from Baptista after the funeral.

23

Baptista didn't want to give them back, but he took them any way. He hadn't felt this destroyed since the death of Sophia. Even the death of his father hadn't effected him like this because he rationalized that was the natural order of things and Carmen's death was not.

At 15 and 13, Taylor and Lorraine didn't care about anything any more. Except for "hi" and "bye", they even quit talking to their Dad.

CHAPTER FIVE

1964

JANUARY

1963 was gone and 1964 was here. There was nothing for Taylor to celebrate because she realized this was the beginning of the first year for the rest of her life without her Mother. Christmas sucked, everything sucked.

Baptista didn't come over to the house that much anymore and that was the way Taylor liked it. When she did come over, it was because she wanted money. Taylor liked seeing her nephews. She could see a little spark return to her Dad's eyes when he played with them. But as far as she was concerned, seeing Baptista at her Grandma's house was enough.

Taylor and Lor went to dances, to the movies and the beach with Van, Tim and the rest of their crowd. They skipped Mass and Lor's job was to run into St. Peter and Paul's back vestibule and grab the church bulletin so they could show it to Big Joe, to prove that they went to Mass. Outside of their house, they acted like normal teenage girls; but when they stepped inside their house, they were motherless children with a father caught up in heartache and sorrow, hiding in his room. More than ever Joe wondered how Aldo just got on with his life, married so soon after Sophia's death and had more children. At the funeral home, Aldo told him that life was for the living, but even though he knew he should want to live for his daughters, he wondered if he died if he would be with Carmen again.

* * *

Chi Chi gave Joe until February to sulk and then she went over to the house and let him have it.

"You have two daughters to raise and right now they are raising themselves," she scolded.

"You think I don't know it? Believe me, Chi Chi, I know it."

"Then get up off your ass, get out of this bedroom and do something about it."

"Don't you understand? If I could, I would."

"Don't I understand? My sister is dead. My mother cries every night for my baby sister. Oh, I understand. It's easier for you to hide in here with your memories than to be out in the real world, suffering with the rest of us."

She sat down on the bed next to him and took his hand.

"I don't know how, Chi Chi. I don't know how," he said looking away from her so she wouldn't see the tears in his eyes. She looked so much like Carmen.

"You take it one step at a time. First do something easy, something you enjoy. What did you like to do for fun that you didn't do with Carmen?"

"On Saturday I played cards at the Italian American."

"Then that will be your first step out into the world but as far as this house goes, you will not hide in your room any longer. Even if you just sit in the living room in front of the TV, you are available to those girls if they need you. Now, I am going to tell Lor and Taylor that if you don't sit in the living room and watch TV and if you don't go to play cards, they are to call me right away and I will be back. Are you listening to me Joe? I will be back and I will bring Mama."

"No, no, not Mama."

26

"Yes, Mama."

Big Joe emerged from his room and sat in his chair in front of the TV. He could hear Chi Chi in the kitchen talking with Taylor and Lor. She could make them laugh, he could not. He looked out the front window into the street. There was a lot of snow. He probably should go shovel off the sidewalk and he would shovel the driveway later. One step at a time.

CHAPTER SIX

1965
A SATURDAY AFTERNOON IN JANUARY

It just happened. Lorraine wasn't home, her Dad was at the Italian American Club playing cards with his buddies and it just happened. It didn't make her feel good, it didn't make her feel bad and except for a twinge of guilt, she didn't feel anything at all. Thanksgiving was terrible and Christmas was worse. She wasn't the good girl virgin any more and her Mom was still dead.

THAT SATURDAY NIGHT

They were sitting in the Warren Theater, eating popcorn, holding a big cup of Coke between their thighs. They'd gotten there early and were watching people choosing their seats and waiting for the movie to start. They always sat on the left, in the first two aisle seats on the end of the very last row, with their backs against the wall. That way nobody could get them from behind and if a fight broke out that they didn't want to join in on, they could make a quick exit through the lobby and out the front door. Fights generally didn't break out inside the theatre; it was when you walked outside you had to watch your back. To the people walking by, it looked like they were having a normal conversation. They weren't yelling, in fact they were as close to whispering as they could get without being considered sissies.

"You son-of-a-bitch, what the hell is wrong with you?" Tim was pissed.

"What's your problem?" Van snapped back. "Don't get bent out of shape. I care about her."

"Don't bullshit a bullshitter. She's just one more scratch mark on your Zippo."

"We quit doing the mall thing didn't we?"

"Get real. You stopped doing the mall thing because I did and you didn't want to go alone. What about Bridges and Fitzpatrick?"

"What about them? They're big girls, they know the score."

"I don't mean what about them like I care about them, you asshole. Taylor doesn't know the score."

"They have seniority."

"Seniority? What the hell do you mean seniority?"

"You know, seniority, I've been with them longer than Taylor, you know, seniority."

"You are fuckin' nuts."

"Who in the hell are you? You don't even have a girlfriend. When is the last time you even had a date?"

"You know why I don't have a girlfriend and why I don't date? I'll tell you why. I'm a bastard and I know it. Oh you've got the charm and you fooled yourself into thinking you're not but you're a bigger son-of-a bitch than me. I'm just honest about it."

"You don't get it. It's my nature. I can't help it. It's like dogs hate cats and cats eat birds. I can't tell you why but it is and you can't go against nature."

"What? It's your nature to whore around so it's okay to screw Taylor and tell me about it because it's your nature?

You've done some fucked up things but this is really fucked up."

"Don't get righteous on me."

"She's been through enough and she's going to get hurt."

"She can't get hurt if she doesn't know and I'm not going to tell her, and you're not going to tell her so she isn't going to get hurt."

"How do you know that Thena or Gwen or one of those other Grandale broads won't tell her? Did you ever think of that? The broads around here are afraid of you but they aren't."

Athena Morningstar Kelly (Thena to her friends), Gwen Shields and her sisters, Jill and Ann, met the guys at a St. Christopher Dance in 1963. It was Grandale meets Warrendale and love at first sight for Gwen and Ted. Thena went out with Wayne and Jill and Ann dated Ted's cousins, Brad and Beau.

"Thena's not going to tell because she doesn't want Taylor to get mad at her. Gwen might, I'll give you that but I'll deal with that if it happens."

"And what about Lor?"

"I'll let you handle her."

"I'm not going to handle her. If she finds out, you deserve what you get but you damn well better watch your back because Thena's brother gave her a switchblade and she will use it."

"What's she going to do, stick me in the back?"

"She's not a backstabber; she'd go right for your dick."

"That's never going to happen. You're acting like a pussy."

"Because I care about what happens to your girlfriend, I'm acting like a pussy? Nice, real nice."

"Man, you worry too much.

"And you don't worry at all. I admit most of the time I don't give a shit but once in a while I do care about something. How do you always just not care?"

"Pay attention because I'm only going to say this once. If I don't like something, I don't do it. If somebody pisses me off, I beat the shit out of them and I know you've got my back and you know I've got your back. I don't have anything to worry about."

There is was again, that little nagging bit of conscience that Tim hated but was afraid if he lost it all together, he would act worse than Van. He knew he had to keep himself under control because he knew he was capable of doing a lot of damage. It made him shutter to think he was the conscience for both of them. That wasn't a good thing.

"You know what you need? You need to get laid."

"How do you know I'm not?"

"Are you?"

"I've thought about it."

"But you like your hand too much," Van laughed.

Hey, I'll take my hand and a Playboy over that pig Fitzpatrick any day," Tim flicked his lit cigarette butt at Van.

"Why do you care so much anyway?"

Tim couldn't tell Van because he thought he was in love with Taylor. At least what he thought love was. He just didn't want Taylor to get hurt but he knew in his gut it was way too late, because the harm was already done.

A Saturday in March

Taylor watched out of her bedroom window for her Dad to back his car out of the driveway and leave for the Italian American before she came downstairs.

"Lor can I come in?" she asked knocking on her bedroom door.

"It's open," Lor answered.

Lorraine was laying in bed in her flannel pajamas and fuzzy slippers reading *True Story*.

"Geez, your room is trashed." There were dirty clothes hanging off the mirror of her triple dresser, empty glasses with dried up Coke residue mixed in with more dirty clothes on the floor.

"You asked to come in here. Lor slid the ashtray out from under her bed and lit a cigarette. "Want one?"

"No thanks."

"If you're going to bitch me out, you can leave."

Taylor sat down on the bed. "I'm sorry. I don't want to fight. I need to talk to you, it's important."

"What's so important?" Lor asked reaching over to turn down her clock radio on the small table next to her bed.

"I think I'm pregnant."

"You're what?"

"Pregnant, knocked up, a bun in the oven."

"You've gone and done it now. Did you go to the doctor?"

"No I didn't go to the doctor, he'd tell Dad."

"Then how do you know for sure?"

"Well I'm late, I'm throwing up, I feel like shit, my boobs hurt and I peed on three tablespoons of Draino in a mason jar and it turned purple." She sat the jar on top of the triple dresser.

"Jesus, Mary and Joseph. What are you going to do?"

"Do, what am I going to do? I'm going to slit my wrists. I don't know what the hell I'm going to do."

"No really, you have to tell Dad."

"Tell Dad, tell Dad!. I only did it one time. Only one time," she said sitting back down on the bed.

"You shouldn't have done it at all."

"No shit. I just need some time to think."

"Think! You should have done that before you fucked Van. It is Van, right?"

"Of course it's Van. I'm not a slut."

"I know. I was hoping you had better taste."

"Nice, Lorraine, real nice."

"Wait don't tell me, let me guess. The rubber broke."

"Well I guess it did. You're a regular Nancy Drew."

"I wish Mom was here."

"If Mom were here, this never would have happened. Don't cry, Lorraine. You weren't home and I was feeling lonely and I really missed Mom and it happened. It's going to be okay. I'll tell Dad. I promise just not now."

Lor put her cigarette out, slid the ashtray back under her bed, ran to the kitchen and grabbed the calendar off the pantry door. They counted from the date of Taylor's last period and figured she was going to have her baby sometime in September. That gave her a few more months before she had to tell her Dad. But what about Van, she didn't know if she wanted to tell him at all but she knew she had to.

A Saturday in April

Taylor met Van at Waysides because she figured if she told him in a public place he wouldn't yell and she just wasn't sure what he was going to do. She had rehearsed the little speech she wanted to make over and over again, except she couldn't decide if she wanted to keep the baby or put it up for adoption. She was sitting there looking out the front window of the little restaurant at the cars driving by on Warren Avenue and playing with her fries, lost in thought.

"What's wrong with you?" Van asked.

"I'm pregnant," she blurted out. So much for working it into the conversation.

"Say that again. I don't think I heard you right," he said dropping his cheeseburger onto the plate.

"I'm pregnant."

"We only did it once." He'd been screwing other girls all the time and they didn't get knocked up. How could she get knocked up when they only did it once?

"Don't you think I know that?"

"We're too young to have a kid."

"We're not having a kid, I am. I'm the one that's knocked up. Everybody's going to know I'm pregnant but they don't have to know you're the father. You can walk

33

around and nobody will point at you and talk behind your back."

"Everybody is going to know it's me. Does Big Joe know?"

"I haven't told him yet."

"He's going to kill me."

"What do you think he's going to do to me? I don't want to get married. I already made one big mistake and I don't want to make another one."

"Me either."

"And I don't want anything from you."

"Look, I'm not going to walk away from you. It's just right now I don't know what to do. Put the kid up for adoption?"

"Well, that's my decision since I'd be the one raising it. It's all going to depend on what happens when I tell my Dad."

"Who knows?"

"My sister."

"I gotta tell Tim and my brother. They won't say anything.

"I know."

They agreed not to tell their parents until they figured out what to do.

A SATURDAY IN MAY

Van stood on Taylor's front porch smoking his cigarette trying to get up his courage to knock on the door. Lor looked out the dinning room window and saw him standing there.

"What do you want?" she asked locking the screen door.

"Is Big Joe home?" Van asked.

"No, he's at the Italian American. Why, you want to talk to my Dad?"

"No, I don't' want to talk to your Dad. I want to talk to Taylor."

"I don't know if she wants to talk to you."

"Would you quit being such a bitch and get your sister."

"Don't you dare come over to my house and cop an attitude with me after what you did to my sister. TAYLOR, ITS HERE."

Taylor came downstairs and stood in front of the screen door.

"What do you want?"

"I need to talk to you alone.

"Where's Tim?"

"He's home. Why do you care where Tim is?"

"He calls me."

"He calls you?"

"Don't you unlock that door," Lor warned.

"I want to hear what he has to say," she said opening the screen door. "You can come in but don't sit down, you won't be staying."

"I said alone, Lorraine."

"This is my house and I'm not leaving you alone with my sister. The last time you were alone with her in my house you knocked her up," Lor shot back.

"She stays. You haven't called me in a week so what's so secret that my sister can't hear it?"

"It's more private than secret."

"Oh please, just say whatever it is."

"You don't have to worry anymore, I solved our problem. I joined the Navy."

"You mean you solved your problem."

"I solved both our problems."

"Really because from where I'm standing you get to leave and I'm still pregnant."

Van didn't tell her that Tim and Wayne went to the recruiter on the same day. Tim enlisted in the Marines and even though Van told Tim he would join the Marines with him, he decided to go Navy with Wayne. He changed his mind because of the stories June Cooper, Ted's Dad, told about being a Sea Bee in World War II and the fact that Ted enlisted in the Navy in 1964, right after he graduated from Cody High School, and he liked it. By the end of summer eight guys within a three block radius became the property of Uncle Sam, including Dave Sullivan who was given the option of enlisting in the Army or going to jail for a long, long time.

SECOND WEEK IN JUNE

Taylor finished out the school year wearing baggy clothes. It wasn't difficult for her to hide her ever increasing belly from her Dad because he really didn't pay that much attention to what they wore. He figured as long as they weren't sick, everything was okay.

FRIDAY NIGHT, THIRD WEEK IN JUNE

Taylor wasn't exactly sure what happened. Tim and Wayne came over and told her and Lor that Van chugged a fifth of Jack Daniels at a birthday party where Tim's band, The Fugitives, was playing and he died. Tim did CPR till the ambulance got there and the Emergency Room doctor said Tim saved Van's life. Van was stable when Tim left the hospital but he had alcohol poisoning and they were keeping him overnight. It seems the human body can't withstand such a rapid intake of high octane booze.

"You should have left him dead," Lor said.

"God, Lorraine, that's cold even for you," Tim said.

"Well, I guess he hasn't solved all his problems."

"I know," Taylor said.

"Too bad Tim knows CPR. The world might be a better place if he didn't. Are you crying?"

"I'm doomed. I'm 16 years old and I'm doomed."

"You're in a jam but you're not doomed. Have the baby and give it up for adoption then you can start all over and you're rid of Van but you have to be rid of Van. If you give up the baby and you're not rid of Van then you are doomed."

This was the first time Tim ever agreed with Lor because he thought if Taylor stayed with Van she would be doomed.

Tim patted Taylor on the back; it was the closest he could come to a comforting gesture. Wayne, who wasn't afraid to show concern, bent down and gave her a hug. He was 6 feet tall, with blonde hair and blue eyes. He carried a switchblade but he'd never pulled it. However, when push came to shove, he'd beaten the crap out of a few guys who mistook the fact that he didn't act like a thug for weakness. He lifted weights every day and he always watched his back and if there was trouble and his brother Al was nearby, he knew Al would pull his knife. Al was like Van and Tim, fuck with him or his brothers and you'd go down hard.

JULY

It was over 90 degrees at Kensington and they knew it was the last time they would all be together like this before the guys left for boot camp and they were having fun. The girls were wearing two piece bathing suits and the guys were in cutoffs. They were running up and down the beach and jumping in and out of the lake, everybody except Taylor. She was sitting in the sand, wearing a sweatshirt and jeans. Lor, Van and Tim would go up and talk to her and then go back to goofing around. Everybody else yelled hello to her when they got there, but she wasn't acting like she wanted to be bothered so they stayed clear.

"I bet she's pregnant," Jill said.

"You don't know that," Thena said.

"It doesn't take Einstein to figure it out," Gwen said.

"Then why is she sitting on the beach dressed like that?" Ann asked.

"You know she doesn't like the water. That's how rumors get started," Thena said.

"Okay, she doesn't like the water but she could still wear a bathing suit or shorts."

"She's sitting in the sand in jeans. You can't tell me you don't think she's knocked up," Jill said.

"Whether she is or she isn't, it's none of our business. I'm going back in the water. If you want to stand there and stare, that's on you," Thena said running back down to the lake.

"What was that all about?" Wayne asked.

"They think Taylor's knocked up," Thena answered.

"Do you?"

"I guess I do I just don't think it's anybody's business. If she is, she has enough trouble she doesn't need us talking about her."

"So we won't," Wayne said dunking her head under the water.

Gwen walked down to the water and stood next to Van. Gwen was a big boned, tall girl and not intimidated by anybody, let alone a piece of shit like Van Thomas.

"You're a prick. You fuck around with those sluts and you knock up the nice girl," Gwen said.

"Kiss my ass," Van replied.

"You know what Thomas, you're the one that's going to be kissing ass in boot camp," she said flipping him off and walking away.

* * *

Tim left for Camp Lejeune, North Carolina and a few days later Van and Wayne left for Great Lakes, Illinois. Sullivan was scheduled to leave for boot camp in Kentucky the following week.

A THURSDAY IN AUGUST

Wearing sweatshirts and Levis in the steamy and humid Detroit heat was getting to be too much for Taylor and sitting in front of a fan that just blew around stagnate hot air wasn't helping anymore. She figured it was time to tell Big

38

Joe because she knew she wouldn't be able to keep this up much longer.

"Dad, can we talk?" Taylor asked.

Lor sat on the couch next to her.

"Dad, first I want to say I'm very sorry. I really am. It just happened. I don't even know how it happened. I mean I was feeling sad about Mom and I felt all alone and . . ."

"What happened? What are you saying to me?"

"What I'm saying is and I'm really sorry but Dad I'm pregnant."

"You are going to have a baby? You are just a child. Is this what you are telling me, that you are going to have a baby?"

"Yes."

"And you know about this?" he looked over at his other daughter.

"Yes," Lor answered.

"I don't understand how such a thing like this could happen. You are a good girl. You are both good girls. You mother, God rest her soul, she taught you better."

"I know," Taylor cried.

"Who is the boy? Is it the Van Thomas boy?"

"Yes."

"Your mother and I welcomed that boy into our home. I fed that boy in my home and he does this to my daughter."

He sat looking out the front window at the street for what seemed like forever to Taylor and Lor, not moving, not talking and when Lor tried to talk to him, he put his open hand up in the air, his signal for don't speak.

"Do his parents know this?" he finally asked.

"No," Taylor answered.

"Who else knows of this?"

"Boone and Tim and Wayne."

"You are sure this is all?"

"Yes."

"And he is off to the Navy. This is a fine mess. I have tried after your mother died to take care of you girls. I have failed."

"You haven't failed, Dad. It's that Van, he's no good," Lor cried.

"Good or bad, we are stuck with him now, aren't we?"

He didn't know how to handle the situation and he didn't know how to ask for help. All he knew to do was go to work and come home but this was not a time for pride; he knew he had to ask for help.

"Both of you sit here. Do not move. I will call Grandma and Chi Chi. They will know what to do. Maybe I call Uncle Carlos too so he can kill him." Carlos was an Army Sniper in World War II with a rifle and a scope he knew would be perfect for the job.

Within the hour, Joe called Evelyn and Bob and told them Taylor was in the family way and they came right over.

With Van in Great Lakes playing sailor, Chi Chi sat on the couch between Taylor and Lor and they listened to the three adults decide Taylor's fate. When Van came home on leave, they would get married. She didn't want to get married. She still didn't know whether she wanted to keep her baby or give it up for adoption but she knew she didn't want to get married. She wasn't old enough to get married. They hadn't even been writing to each other. Tim wrote her but Van didn't. She wished her mother was there. If her mother was alive, she wouldn't be in this mess. Chi Chi reached over and held Taylor's hand. The decision was made. Taylor was overwhelmed and scared; but she didn't protest.

SEPTEMBER

Taylor had only seen the doctor twice before she gave birth to a happy, healthy baby girl. She named her Sarah Elizabeth and because Van was still at Great Lakes and they weren't married, the place for "father's name" on Sarah's

Birth Certificate was left blank until Van came home and acknowledged paternity. So for the time being, her baby's name was Sarah Elizabeth Ginetti.

Years later, when Taylor asked Thena if she knew she was pregnant with Sarah, Thena replied, "Nobody goes to the beach and sits in the sand wearing a sweatshirt and jeans. That was the tip off."

* * *

Van got home from Boot Camp the end of September and after dropping his duffel bag off at his parents' house, headed straight over to see Taylor and the baby. His parents wrote him and told him that he was marrying Taylor and that was that. He thought about skipping his 30 days at home and going somewhere else but he just couldn't do it to Taylor and now he had a kid.

When Taylor put Sarah in his arms, he immediately fell in love, "She's beautiful."

"Of course you think she's beautiful, she looks just like you," Taylor said.

"What do you want to do?"

"If you stay home, I don't have a choice, I have to marry you."

"And if I leave?"

"There's only one way to find out."

"I can't run out on you."

"You can't because I think you already did."

"That's not fair."

"You are the kind of guy that would chew his foot off to get out of a trap."

"I'm here aren't I?"

"Why are you here?"

"She's my kid too. This isn't what either one of us wanted but it happened, it is what it is and I think we need to get married and make the best of it. It's not like we don't care about each other and we don't know each other. I got my orders to California, you and the baby can move with me. It wouldn't be so bad living in California, would it?"

41

"I guess right now any place would be better than here. I can't stand the hurt look in my Dad's eyes. He quit looking at us when my Mom died and back then I wanted him to look at me but now he looks at me and it kills me."

"My parents are pretty pissed off at me too, mostly Evelyn, but I'm just passing through. Evelyn thinks she's too young to be a grandma."

"Poor Evelyn," Taylor said sarcastically.

"And she's pissed you named her Sarah Elizabeth. She says she gave you a list of "V" names."

"And what about you, are you pissed?"

"Hell, no. I know Evelyn isn't perfect. Can you roll with that?"

"I think I can roll with anything."

OCTOBER

A week before Van left for California, Taylor and Van were married in a private ceremony in chambers by Wayne County Probate Court Judge Joseph Alcini attended only by their parents, Lorraine and Boone. Because Taylor was a minor, that's the way it had to be. Joe played cards with Judge Alcini at the Italian American and he handled Sarah's adoption too. Sarah Elizabeth Ginetti's Birth Certificate would be forever sealed by the State of Michigan and unavailable to anybody but Taylor. She was now officially Sarah Elizabeth Thomas.

NOVEMBER

As soon as Van rented an apartment off base in San Diego, Taylor packed up her and Baby Sarah and bought an airplane ticket with money Van sent her. San Diego was the largest naval base on the West Coast and the principal homeport of the Pacific Fleet.

Taylor loved California the minute she got off of the plane. It was like paradise with the Pacific Ocean, palm trees and the sun was shinning. There wouldn't be any snow and ice storms here. She was starting a new life.

DECEMBER

Other than missing her family, Christmastime in California was wonderful. When Van came home from the base at the end of the day, she would have dinner ready and they would take Sarah for a walk in her stroller.

The decks of the ships that were in port were decorated with Christmas lights and the aircraft carrier even had a Christmas tree. The waterfront was aglow with a long row of battle ship grey Navy ships of all sizes with red and green lights reflecting on the water.

Van was training to be a Sea Bee and Taylor knew that meant he would be going to Viet Nam, but she just wanted to enjoy the moment. They'd gotten two letters, one from Tim saying that he would be going to Nam in February and one from Ted who was already in Nam.

CHAPTER SEVEN

1966

Taylor had been in San Diego for two months and she kept pinching herself because she couldn't believe Van actually picked out the great apartment they were living in. Even though it was a simple two bedroom apartment with a living room, dinette and small kitchen, it was a palace to her. They lived on the second floor with a balcony that overlooked the pool. Mostly Navy families lived in the apartment complex and Taylor easily made friends with the other wives. In the afternoon they sat around the pool, talked, laughed and played with their babies. At home she was the "bad girl" but in San Diego, she was just another sailor's wife and most of the other wives had the same story she did, knocked up, got married and left town.

She was cautiously optimistic at how responsible Van had become. If he didn't have to stay on base, he came straight home. He liked the Navy and she was beginning to think that their marriage might actually work out and she knew it was because they got out of Warrendale. Then Van got his orders to Viet Nam. They had a little while before he had to leave because he was still training and then she was pregnant again. She couldn't believe it, Sarah wouldn't even be a year old by the time this baby was born and Van would be gone again.

"Babe, you need to go back home," Van said.

"I don't want to go back home. I like it here. We can live here in the apartment until you come back."

"And what if I don't come back?"

"Don't talk like that."

"So my fate has been decided again."

"I know I can't make you go back home if you don't want to so no your fate hasn't been decided again, but I think it's the best thing for all of us if you do. If I don't get stationed in California when I get back from Nam, we can move here after I get out."

"Will you promise me that we won't live in Detroit when you get out?"

"Yes, I do promise you we won't live in Detroit when I get out."

* * *

Big Joe had a lot to think about since Van called and his mind was working overtime. He knew they all thought he didn't know what was going on and until a very pregnant Taylor told him she was going to have a baby, he had to admit to himself he didn't. It wasn't that he didn't care, it was that he was submerged into his own suffering and grief so much that he forgot how to care about anything else but since Taylor's announcement, he paid attention.

He knew that after Taylor moved to California, Lorraine got a diamond engagement ring from a boy six years older than her. She hid the ring from him but he knew. He was worried that she would get pregnant, then what would he do? Chi Chi told him Lorraine knew better but he thought Taylor knew better and she didn't. He was relieved when the boy got drafted. He knew Lorraine wrote to him and that was okay because he was on the other side of the world and he hoped he would be there for at least a year. She wasn't dating anybody that he knew of, she was getting good grades in school but she still didn't talk to him all that much and she stayed in her room. Maybe when Taylor got home and after Lorraine got her driver's license and he gave her Taylor's Mustang, things would change and she would like him again.

Taylor was coming home with Sarah and another baby on the way. He liked the idea of them living with him but he didn't want Van in his house and he didn't want Taylor living with Evelyn. He couldn't stand being in the same room with the woman. And what would happen when Van came home on leave? He didn't want the boy to get hurt in Viet Nam but he didn't want him back home either. When Van called he said Taylor and the baby could spend a week with him and Lorraine and then a week at Evelyn's house. This was his daughter and his granddaughter. He didn't want them spending one day at that woman's house let alone one week. The mere thought of them spending any time with Evelyn made him cringe.

He played his Saturday card games at the Italian American with Judge Alcini and the rest of his buddies but instead of going home, he stopped at Chi Chi's house to talk with her and Carlos. There had to be a solution to this problem and he hoped they would help him find one.

"Buy her a house," Chi Chi said. She looked so much like Carmen that sometimes it was difficult for him to look at her, but she thought like Carmen too and that is what he had to focus on.

"She can't take care of a house with two babies."

"So buy her a house by you," Carlos said. Carlos had a full head of thick black hair, dark eyes and a no nonsense attitude, however, in most family matters, he deferred to his Mama and Chi Chi and unless he had strong feelings to the contrary, went along with whatever plan they devised. He was a couple inches taller than Big Joe, which didn't make him all that tall but Big Joe looked up to him and loved him like a brother and the feeling was mutual.

"But I don't want him to have the house," Joe said.

"We said buy *her* a house," Chi Chi repeated.

"Oh, so I buy the house for her but I keep it in my name because when she gets rid of him, and I know she will, he can't take it from her."

"Now you're cookin'."

"And she needs a car," Carlos said.

"You could give her the Mustang," Chi Chi added.

"No, I will get her a car but she cannot have the Mustang. The Mustang is Lorraine's."

"You mean that Mustang that is parked in front of my house, that Mustang?"

"Chi Chi, leave him alone. He can drive the car. He bought it," Carlos interjected.

"Are you punishing her?" Chi Chi asked.

"No, I'm not punishing her. How can I punish her for what is my fault?"

"You can't blame yourself."

"I will always blame myself. Lorraine blames me. She won't even talk to me and she stays in her room."

"She's a teenage girl. Her sister left her. Her mother died. Your wife died. Our sister died. It is not your fault."

"I know what he means, Chi Chi. He feels like he didn't protect her," Carlos said.

"I don't agree with the way you men think. So he protects her now. Joe, you find a house. Carlos you find a car and Mama and I will get furniture. We all have extra furniture."

"But will she agree? What if she doesn't want a house?" Joe asked.

"You two sit here and be quiet," Chi Chi said. "Taylor, honey, how are you and my precious baby Sarah?"

"Aunt Chi Chi we're doing good. I love California. Did you hear that Van got his orders to Nam and he wants me to move back home?"

"Yes I did hear and that's why I'm calling. Where do you plan to live when you get back here?"

"Van has this plan that I switch off weeks between his house and my house but I don't much like the idea. To tell you the truth, I don't want to come back."

"Now, honey, you have to come back that is not an option. You can't be that far away with two babies. You know that don't you?"

"I guess. It's just that everything is so nice out here. The sun shines all the time and I've made friends here. I am afraid to come back."

"You don't need to be afraid; your family is here to help you. Honey, you know all the friends you made are there temporarily just like you. When their husbands get transferred to another place, they will be leaving too, just like you need to leave and come home. I have an idea. I think you should have your own house. Not too big of a house. Just a nice little house for you and your family."

"We can't afford a house."

"Your Daddy can."

"I can't ask him to buy me a house after what I did to him."

"You didn't do anything to him. You are his little girl. I don't know why this family thinks they have to blame themselves for everything."

"Why, doesn't he want me to stay at home?"

"Oh, he wants you to stay with him but he doesn't want you to stay with Van's people. Let me tell you a little secret, he doesn't like them very much."

Big Joe shook his head and Chi Chi waved her hand in the air for him to chill.

"She knows what she is doing," Carlos whispered.

"You leave it to Aunt Chi Chi, I will talk to your Daddy about buying you a house."

"What if Van gets stationed in California. I want to live in California."

"So we sell the house. Taylor, if your mother were here I know this is what she would want you to do."

48

"Bringing up Mom isn't playing fair you know. I'll talk to Van."

"Talk to him all you want but your Daddy is buying you a house. Grandma and I will find furniture and I know Uncle Carlos will look around for a nice car. No tears now. Everything is going to be okay."

"It's just that this is the first time since my Mom died that I feel like I am not alone."

"Honey, you were never alone. We have always been here for you. You just forgot for a while. Now you dry your eyes and give Sarah a big hug and kiss from her Great Aunt Chi Chi."

"You are a great aunt."

"Now, you are going to make me cry. You will be home before you know it."

"I love you."

"I love you too."

"Tell Dad and Uncle Carlos they did good keeping their mouths shut this long."

"Goodbye smarty pants," Chi Chi laughed and hung up the phone.

"Well, what did she say?" Big Joe asked.

"She was on to us but she agreed. Our babies are coming home."

* * *

In May of 1966, Van was on his way to Viet Nam and Taylor was on a plane with Sarah sitting on her ever growing pregnant lap and Chauncey, Van's pet baby boa constrictor, stuffed into the diaper bag. She was glad they got a direct flight because she stuck two baby bottles and a couple diapers in her purse and if she needed more than that she had a problem because she wasn't putting her hand into the diaper bag for anything. It was bad enough that the top of the diaper bag didn't zip shut and she had to keep both of her feet flat on top of the diaper bag during the entire flight. Evelyn and Bob were picking them up at Metro Airport where she would hand the diaper bag over to her father-in-

49

law who would deposit Chauncey into his temporary new aquarium at her in-laws' house.

"He kept constructing and the top kept popping up and I had to keep pushing my feet back down," she told Thena.

"What the hell, are you nuts? If that snake got out and I was on the plane, I would have had a heart attack," Thena said.

"I wasn't going to let him get out."

"I don't know why I believe you but I do."

* * *

Joe bought a small two bedroom bungalow for his daughter and granddaughter six blocks from Evelyn and Bob and less than 5 minutes away from him and Lorraine. He also bought her a used Ford Fairlane. He was driving the Mustang until Lorraine turned 16 in September and then he was giving it to her. It bothered Taylor that Lor was getting her burgundy Mustang with the black vinyl roof that she picked out, but at the same time, she understood.

* * *

In July their first son, baby Vance was born. Sarah and Vance both had Van's blonde hair and Taylor's brown eyes. Lor learned in her high school Biology Class that blonde hair and brown eyes were a rare combination because blondes statistically have blue eyes. Other than their brown eyes, Sarah and Vance were all Thomas.

CHAPTER EIGHT

1967
JUNE

Taylor's house was the neighborhood hangout for a select few. They smoked cigarettes, watched TV or listened to the radio and at night they brought liquor and engaged in moderate social drinking. They liked to play Black Jack and at the end of the game, they gave all the money in the pot to Taylor to help her pay her utility bills. Taylor was either the dealer or she sat on the couch watching the game depending on if the kids were awake or asleep.

Evelyn did her daily drop in unannounced visits at different times of the day or night. Somebody always sat in the lookout chair next to the front door but there was a spy on the inside and they knew it.

Vita was a big boned girl, bigger than Boone and almost as big as Van, next to petite Lorraine, Thena and Taylor she looked even bigger than she really was. The only thing bigger on Vita than her body, was her mouth. Of Evelyn's six kids, Boone and Vita were the only ones that had brown hair and brown eyes, all the others had blonde hair and blue eyes. While most girls, including Thena, were bleaching their hair blonde, Lorraine died her hair auburn and Taylor didn't see any reason to mess with the dark hair that Mother Nature gave her.

Vita would do anything to earn her mother's approval plus she didn't like Thena or Lorraine and the feeling was mutual. It wasn't uncommon for one sarcastic remark to erupt into nasty verbal onslaughts and all the while Taylor would sit quietly, smoking her cigarette but when the insults got a little too close to bitch slapping, she'd send Vita packing and that really pissed Evelyn off. This particular Saturday night in June was no exception.

"How dare you make my daughter leave her brother's house," Evelyn admonished after an altercation of immense proportion that even caused the usually unflappable Coldicott brothers, Marty and Jack, to cut their Black Jack game short and flee.

"Her brother's house? Did you just say 'her brother's house'? This is my father's house, Evelyn, not her brother's house. In fact, Evelyn, tell Vita I don't want her coming over here any more unless she calls me first. That goes for you too," Taylor said hanging up the phone.

"I can't believe you told the old bitty off," Lor said.

"I don't want any trouble with her but she can't keep bulldozing her way into my life plus send her flying monkey in here to do her bidding. I'm sick of it."

"Her whole life is Van and he's gone, she has no control over him so now it's you and the kids," Thena said.

"She never had any control over him," Lor said.

"But she thought she did."

"If she only knew how he really felt about her. I don't want to get to the point where I tell her he doesn't give a damn about her. I have no use for her but I don't want to hurt her feelings either," Taylor interjected.

"She'd carve you up in a heartbeat," Lor said.

"And she'd dance on your grave," Thena added.

"I know but I'm not going to lower myself to be like her. She is my kids' Grandmother."

52

THURSDAY AFTERNOON, JULY 20TH

Tim was home on leave from Nam. He was wearing a white tank top and blue jeans, the white looked good against his Viet Nam tan. He was damn fine looking in his Marine uniform, Thena thought, but he looked just like ordinary Tim in his civies. They were sitting across from each other in the olive green upholstered arm chairs that matched the couch, in Taylor's living room. Thena was in the lookout chair.

Tim and Thena were scared, close to cardiac arrest status, of snakes. In fact, neither Tim nor Thena would step foot into Taylor's house unless she crossed her heart and hoped to die that Chauncey was on lockdown in his aquarium. They were having one of their usual smack down conversations when Thena's right eye began to twitch and all the color drained from her face.

"What Miss Smartass, the cat got your tongue?" Tim asked gearing up to really start ragging on her.

"Ah ah . . ."

"I see my extreme intelligence has rendered you speechless or perhaps it is my uncommon good looks. Why are your eyes all spastic?"

Her eyes were darting back and forth from the floor to Tim.

"I, it . . ."

"I, it? What the hell is that? Say something I can understand why don't you? I thought you Catholic school girls were smart."

Thena heard every word he was saying and she really wanted to hurt him but the words just wouldn't come out because she was otherwise occupied watching the boa constrictor slithering across the floor, between the wall and the back of Tim's chair then winding his way up the leg of the end table. She slowly raised her right arm, careful not to draw the snake's attention to her, and pointed her index finger in the direction of Chauncey, wrapping his body around the lamp.

"What the hell is wrong with you?" Tim said following the direction of Thena's finger with his eyes and at that exact moment, Chauncey tightened his coils around the lamp, stretched his neck and thrust his head out at Tim and they were nose to nose. Thena let out a scream so loud it should have broken glass, grabbed her purse up off of the floor and ran out the front door with Tim running right behind her. They ran across the street and Tim fell down on the curb next to Thena trying to catch his breath.

"Why didn't you tell me?" he gasped.

"Oh don't even go there," Thena cried out, holding her right hand over her pounding heart. "I tried to tell you but nothing came out."

"Since when can't you talk?"

"When I see a snake! I pointed didn't I? What more do you want from me?"

"And you ran out and left me there."

"What did you expect me to do, save you? You're the big, brave Marine. Hey, I didn't know Marines ran. Wait, what do they call it, retreat?"

"Well you sure as hell aren't having trouble talking now."

"The next time I can't talk maybe that should be your clue that something is wrong."

"Your scream scared the snake. He's clinging to the lamp. You guys okay?" Taylor laughed.

"Do we look okay?" Thena yelled.

"Actually you look kind of cute sitting next to each other like that. With all that heavy breathing, somebody might get the wrong idea."

"Not funny. I think I'm having a heart attack."

"I called Bob, he's on his way over to put Chauncey back. Van should have named him Houdini. Guess we have to put a rock or something on the top of the aquarium to keep him in."

"Ya think."

"You said he was on lock down," Tim yelled.

"I really thought he was. I wouldn't lie to you about that," Taylor replied still laughing.

I'm outta here," Tim said.

"Me too."

They both got in their cars and were gone like the wind.

SUNDAY, JULY 23RD

The Detroit cops raided an after hours blind pig on the corner of 12th Street and Clairmount on Detroit's Westside. The cops expected to find a small crowd inside, but instead there were surprised by over 80 people partying with two Vets who just returned from Viet Nam. A crowd gathered outside and watched the cops loading the partiers into police cars and after the last of the cop cars pulled away, the riot began with broken windows and escalated into violence and looting. The local news didn't report what was going on because the powers that be were hoping it would be localized and not spread to other parts of the City. They didn't have enough manpower so the cops on duty watched the violence, arrested only a few of the rioters and hoped the violence would die down on its own.

It was noon and Thena was standing behind her cash register at K-Mart. Al was home on leave and the only way he could talk to her was to buy something. The first time he chose a picture frame.

"What time do you get off of work?"

Thena looked out the store's front window and saw Beau and his new steady girlfriend, Barb, sitting in his blue, 66' jacked up Chevy Super Sport in the parking lot.

"Five o'clock but the store is really slow so maybe they will let some of us off early. What are you going to do with a picture frame?"

"Return it. We're going to Kensington, see if you can get off work now . I'll be back."

Thena asked her Manager for the rest of the day off and was told to wait and see if business picked up.

This time Al had a bag of pistachios.

"I asked and he said to wait and see if business picks up."

"Don't cry," Al said. "I am going to go talk to Beau, I'll be back."

Just as Al walked out the front door of the store, twelve black people in two cars pulled up in the parking lot, ran into the store and down the middle aisle smashing dishes and turning over displays. Security tried to stop them and the Detroit cops were called.

Al ran back into the store and this time came though her line empty handed.

"Come on, you are getting out of here."

"Kelly, you can leave," her Manager said.

Al grabbed her hand and she ran out the door with him, still wearing her K-Mart smock and glasses. They drove the 3 blocks to Thena's house so she could change her clothes. She put her two piece bathing suit on under her shorts and shirt, grabbed her shades and a towel and they headed the 30 plus miles out to the beach.

Instead of the violence dying down, it escalated so a curfew was set and the public had to be told. At 5:30PM Kensington Metro cops drove through the park with bullhorns announcing that anybody that lived in Detroit had to leave because of a curfew; there was a riot in Detroit. Al and Thena went looking for Beau and Barb who had wandered off and found them over the hill, lying on a blanket making out.

"We've got to go," Al said.

"Why?" Beau asked, looking up over his shoulder at Al and Thena.

"Riots in Detroit. We've go to go." Beau and Barb didn't live in Detroit, but Al and Thena did.

On the way home cars filled with black people kept speeding passed them on the freeway and since Beau was known for his lead foot, they figured the cars passing them were going at least 90 miles an hour.

"All the radio is saying is there is a curfew," Barb said as she channel surfed.

They decided to stay at Thena's house until they figured out what was going on. Sitting around the kitchen table, Mr. & Mrs. Kelly told them about the 1943 Detroit riot and how they watched tanks rolling down their street from their apartment window.

"It was something I didn't think I would ever see again," her Mom said.

"You think there are going to be tanks on the streets?" Thena asked.

"Probably," her Dad answered.

MONDAY, JULY 24TH

Michigan State Troopers were called in to help the Detroit cops and the arrests began. Buildings were set on fire and snipers were shooting at the firemen trying to put them out. Governor George Romney sent in the Michigan National Guard. The sale of guns, ammunition and alcohol was banned but guns and ammo were looted from stores so the violence continued.

Tim was due to leave for Nam on Tuesday but he called the Recruiter and said there was rioting on the corner of his street and he needed to protect his widowed mother. The rioting was still a few miles away but nobody knew if it would continue to spread. He was in no hurry to go back to Nam and who could blame him. Tim's leave was extended two weeks. Ted was in the second day of his 30 day leave. Ted and Gwen were still together; Thena and Al were a new item, and believe it or not, so were Lorraine and Tim.

Lefty and Vi, owners of the local Grandale Mom and Pop store, were selling beer to their friends and regular customers so the ban on alcohol wasn't an issue for Thena's parents and either was ammo and guns. Thena's Dad loaded his 22 rifle and laid it on the floor next to the couch. She shot his 410 rifle for the first time when she was 8 years old and had been watching him clean his guns since she was three, handing him the gun oil, cloth and rod to clean the barrels.

"Athena, you're sleeping on the couch till this is over. Anybody comes up on the porch or in the yard and you don't know them, you shoot," her Dad ordered.

"And nobody touches my new aluminum siding," her Mom added.

These instructions would have scared the average 16 year old girl, but not Athena. She would do what had to be done because she was more afraid of what would happen to her if she didn't.

TUESDAY, JULY 25TH

President Johnson sent in Federal troops from Selfridge Air Force base in Mt. Clemens. Tanks were patrolling the Detroit streets at the core of the rioting, trying to prevent it from spreading out to other neighborhoods. The tanks hadn't come down their streets, but the National Guard in their Jeep vehicles and trucks were there.

Jill, Ann and Thena stood at the end of their street, watching the plumes of smoke rising across the not so far away sky and listening to the echoes of the sirens. At 18, 17 and 16 respectively, they were aware of the National Guardsmen sitting a half a block behind them in a Jeep guarding the corners of Southfield and Plymouth Roads. They could leave their neighborhood without a problem but to get back home, they had to show I.D. They found that out the hard way the night before when they came home from Ted's house after curfew. They were lucky a little flirting got them through the check point and not arrested.

"They say it is a race riot but they are hurting their own people. I don't get it," Thena said.

"As long as they don't hurt us," Ann said.

"It isn't just burning and stealing, people are dead. Do you think it will get to us?" Jill asked.

"Not with the National Guard sitting there."

"Listening to LBJ talk about it on TV scared me," Thena said.

"Listening to LBJ scares you but shooting somebody doesn't?" Jill asked.

"Oh, it scares me but I'm more afraid of my parents if I don't shoot. Other than making cars, I didn't think LBJ even knew we were here."

"Everybody knows where we are now."

The riot raged on for five hot, humid, steamy days and they never did understand why. While the heart of Detroit burned, the riot never got a far as Warrendale and Grandale so they cautiously went on with their lives, ever mindful of the smoke, curfew and National Guard.

SEPTEMBER

Van had a 30 day leave and by the time he returned for his second tour in Nam, Taylor was pregnant again.

* * *

Chi Chi noticed the growing worry clouding Joe's eyes. She knew he was afraid for Taylor and that the memory of Sophia's death was once again fresh in his mind. For months she patted his hand and reassured him that what happened to Sophia wouldn't happen to Taylor. These were different times with modern medicine and doctors. But deep in his heart he knew that modern medicine and modern doctors couldn't stop the Angel of Death if he wanted to claim a soul, the loss of his beloved Carmen was proof of that.

CHAPTER NINE

1968
JUNE

When the plane landed in San Diego, the MP's were waiting
to arrest Van. It never occurred to him that the MP's would
be waiting for him. The fight took place In-Country months
before but the Navy thought it would be bad for morale to
lock him up in Nam. There was a Military Tribunal and the
Sea Bees in his Battalion testified Van was provoked, but
that didn't matter. Maybe if he hadn't broken the
Lieutenant's jaw, his sentence would have been lighter. But
it probably wouldn't have made any difference because the
Lieutenant was a prick, that's why he hit him. So there he
sat in the brig for three months with his wife and kids back
home in Detroit. It could have been worse though, he
would get a general and not a dishonorable discharge.

He had a lot of time to think. Navy Seals were the
number 1 bad boys and the Sea Bee's were number 2. They
were the Navy's builders and fighters and they had to be
tough. He promised himself that when he got home, no
more bad boy and he would do things differently. He'd
control his temper. He'd quit screwing around. He'd make

his marriage work. He loved his kids and he really wanted to be a good father. His father was away from home too much and he swore he would be there for his kids. The Navy taught him how to build roads, bridges and buildings and he was sure he could find a construction job. If not, he'd work on the line. That was the advantage of living in Detroit, you could always find work on the line.

They let Van make one phone call to Taylor.

"Don't tell Evelyn," he said.

"She's going to find out."

"Let her find out but don't tell her. I can't deal with her shit. How do you feel?"

"Fat."

"They said you can call me after the baby is born." Taylor wrote down the phone number and said goodbye. She waddled over to her couch and dropped down on the worn out cushions. She was due any day.

"Was that Van?" Lorraine asked.

"Yes," Taylor answered.

"Is he coming home?"

"In 90 days."

* * *

Tim finished his second tour of duty in Nam and was a Drill Sergeant at Camp Jejune tormenting the new recruits that were unfortunate enough to end up in his Platoon. These were his last bunch and he was counting the days until he was free, 29 days short, 28 days short, 27 days short. When he was in Boot Camp, Jill sent him a Zippo lighter with a naked lady on both sides that she bought at the State Fair and his D.I. put a metal pot over his head, banged on it fifty times with a spoon and then took the lighter, the SOB. His ears rang for hours. That's how he wanted every guy that left his Platoon to remember him, as the no good SOB that made their ears ring. Instead of mellowing at the thought of these being the last guys he would train, he was enjoying his power for the last time. There was always one guy he picked on more than the rest. One he would torture

61

with "give me 50 more" or make run more laps than the other guys. In this group of guys he found one he thought was a pretty boy and showed him no mercy. He found out almost too late that pretty boy was a soon-to-be-visiting-camp Senator's son. So he did the only thing he did better than being a prick, he turned on the charm. The guys back home didn't nickname him "The Entertainer" for nothing. He told the kid he'd been so hard on him because he didn't want the other guys to think he was giving him special treatment because of Daddy. He was going off into combat with these guys and they had to have his back. He gave the kid a smoke, talked a little more, said Semper Fi and the kid bought it. Of course, when Daddy came to visit, Tim once again turned on the charm. After all, he didn't want to get busted down to private when he was so close to being discharged and it was, of course, all about him.

* * *

Thena graduated from Rosary High School and Lorraine graduated from Cody High School on June 6, 1968, the same day baby Vanessa was born and a day after Bobby Kennedy died.

* * *

Taylor wanted Lorraine to pick her up from the hospital but Evelyn insisted and Taylor was too worn out and didn't have the strength to argue. She had three babies in a little over three years all alone. She watched other fathers oohing and aahing over their babies and she told herself this was the life that was chosen for her, she accepted it but she wondered why fate and God hated her so much.

"You can come home with me that way the girls can see the new baby," Evelyn said.

"No thanks, just drop me at my Dad's," Taylor said dreading what was going to come out of Evelyn's mouth next because she could tell by her tone something was up.

"A letter I sent Van came back. They said his address is no good," Evelyn announced.

"Maybe he's in combat and they can't find him," after the words left Taylor's lips she knew she'd made a big mistake.

"Oh my God, he's MIA."

"I didn't say that." Taylor kept looking at Vanessa because she didn't dare look at Evelyn.

"He's hurt, I know it. A mother knows these things. I'm calling the Red Cross."

Taylor was pissed that Van didn't want to deal with Evelyn but he didn't care if she had to.

"He's safe."

"I am his mother. I have a right to know where my son is."

"Really, Evelyn, where is Boone?"

"He's in Korea."

"He's in Japan, Evelyn. Boone is in Japan."

"Korea, Japan, they are all the same to me. Is Van in Korea with Boone?"

"I give up; no Van is not in Japan. Why would you think that?"

"Because you asked me about Boone."

"I was trying to make a point. Van is in the States and he asked me not to tell you where he is. He'll be home in a few weeks.

You know, Evelyn, I've always wondered why all your kids' names start with "V" except Boone's?"

"His middle name is Victor. He got his "V". I don't know what the hell that has to do with anything. Sarah doesn't have a "V" now does she and whose fault is that?

Van is on a secret mission isn't he? That's why he told you not to tell me."

"You guessed it Evelyn. We can't fool you." She really wanted to yell *he's in the Brig* but she didn't.

Lorraine, with Sarah and Vance in tow, picked Taylor and Vanessa up at Evelyn's house.

"Why didn't the old bat bring you to Dad's?" Lorraine asked.

"Because she's calling all of her friends telling them that Van is on a secret mission," Taylor answered.

"Secret mission, what did you tell her?"

"I didn't tell her anything. He said not to tell her where he was so I didn't but you know Evelyn, she knows everything. She's telling people he's a Seal."

"Daddy's not a seal, Daddy's in the Brig," Sarah said proudly.

Taylor looked at Lorraine and they burst out laughing.

VAN AND TIM

By October, Van and Tim were both home. They were still friends, but their lives were going in different directions. Van was not adjusting well to civilian life and he picked right up where he left off with Jayne and Maureen. He'd get a job and work for a month or two and quit. He even got a good paying job on the line at Fisher Body and that didn't last. Tim entered the Detroit Police Academy. Since that's how he talked himself out of the beat down by the Big 4, a squad car manned with 4 of Detroit's finest that patrolled the streets of the 48227 and 48228 with weapons and brute force keeping the natives in line. He told them he was going into the Marines and when he got home he wanted to be a Detroit cop so he figured why not give it a shot? Even though Van and Tim eventually drifted further and further apart they still had two things in common, alcohol and Taylor.

CHAPTER TEN

Taylor dropped the kids off with Lorraine so she could go to the grocery store in peace. It was a sunny afternoon, the kind people look forward to after a long Michigan winter. Van was working at a small shop on Fitzpatrick Court and Taylor wanted to take what little extra money they had and buy groceries before he quit. The frustrating thing was he never got fired, he just up and quit. When she pulled up in the driveway and got out of the car their cat, named Gookie by Sarah, was sitting in the living room window screeching and Van's car was parked out front.

"What's wrong with you, you crazy cat?" She opened the front door and screamed, dropped the grocery bags on the floor and ran to Van. He was face down on the floor and she was sure he was dead. She knelt down beside him, put both her hands on his side and rolled him over onto his back. She put her ear next to his mouth. He was unconscious but he was still breathing. She checked his body for blood but didn't find any and she grabbed him by the shoulders and shook him as hard as she could.

"What did you do?" she cried slapping his face.

He groaned, and an empty plastic Vicodin vial rolled out of his hand.

"You took all of them? Why you selfish son-of-a-bitch?" she called Tim and it seemed like she just hung up the phone and he was running in the front door.

"We'll take him to emergency; by the time an ambulance gets here we could have him there. Grab his ankles," Tim said grabbing Van under the arms and shouldering most of his weight. They threw him in the backseat of Taylor's car. Tim was worried about Van but he didn't want him dying in his brand new GTO.

"Throw me your keys. I'll drive so you can sit back there with him," Tim said.

"You can drive but I'm not sitting back there with him. You're such an asshole," Taylor cried.

Van moaned and Taylor turned up the radio.

"Just handle today and don't worry about tomorrow. That's one thing I learned in Nam."

"And what about tomorrow?"

"What about it?"

"If you don't worry about today or tomorrow, why in the hell do you drink so much?"

"I don't want to remember." Taylor was the only one Tim would be serious with, she was the only one he trusted, he hadn't even shared that with his sisters, his brother or his mother.

Years later, when Tim and Thena were drinking at Zenia's and he was in the bag he told her when he was on patrol in the jungle they were ambushed and the guy next to him was killed. He was shot in the head. The only guy he every let himself make friends with over there. When he heard shots, he looked over and the guy's head was blown off. He looked so serious when he said it, she thought he was telling the truth. Since he never talked about Nam and

66

he was such a bs'er, Thena didn't know if he was blowing smoke or telling her the truth and as much as she wanted to know, she never brought it up again.

"I'm sorry," Van whispered.

"You sure as hell are," Taylor said.

Oakwood Hospital pumped Van's stomach and kept him for observation. There were no statistics on issues with returning Viet Nam Vets and Agent Orange wasn't even in the diagnostic mix then. Dr. Eugene Simon was assigned Van's case and before he would release Van, he asked to meet with Taylor and Evelyn insisted on being there too.

Friday the 13th

Taylor and Evelyn sat in the comfortable, burgundy leather chairs in front of Dr. Simon's equally impressive mahogany desk. Framed diplomas lined the one wall and huge leather bound medical books filled shelves on the other. She looked over at Evelyn and for the first time noticed how all the alcohol she'd drank over the years had ravaged her face and wondered if her hands were shaking because she was nervous or she needed a drink.

"I knew your mother. She was a brilliant nurse. I am glad I finally got the chance to meet you but I am sorry these are not the best of circumstances" Dr. Simon said hoping to put Taylor at ease.

"Thank you. She was a brilliant mother too," Taylor said.

"That being said, I believe your husband . . ."

"He is my son doctor, my son," Evelyn interrupted while she tapped her long, jagged, unpolished fingernails on the arm of the leather chair.

"Yes, I am well aware of that Mrs. Thomas and there is no need to raise your voice. Let me rephrase, Van suffers from manic depression." He had white hair and kind eyes. His years of experience made him compassionate and understanding and he had a knack for being able to recognize the true worth of people and he wasn't impressed with Evelyn.

"There was nothing wrong with my son before he went to Viet Nam."

Taylor looked out the window Dr. Simon was sitting in front of and wondered what it would be like to be able to just enjoy the sunny day instead of sitting next to Evelyn in a shrink's office.

"That's not true," Taylor said.

"That is the truth and you need to keep quiet. You don't understand him. You're the reason he's here. If you hadn't of gotten pregnant and now he is saddled with three kids."

"Mrs. Thomas, I don't want to have to remind you again to lower your voice," Dr. Simon ordered.

"Oh, that's right Evelyn, I knocked myself up. You're going to 'understand him' right into his grave. Your precious son tried to kill himself. Now shut up and let the doctor talk," Taylor said.

"I am his mother."

"That's getting real old, Evelyn. Legally, I'm in charge. I am his next of kin. Isn't that right Dr. Simon?"

"That's right," Dr. Simon smiled. He was sure Van suffered trauma in Viet Nam but that he suffered more trauma over the years at the hands of his mother.

"And if I want her out of the room, she's out."

"Right again."

"Do you get it, Evelyn? I am done with your tantrums and your orders. I'm done with you bringing a steak dinner over to my house for Van and ignoring me and the kids. If you open your mouth one more time, just one more time Evelyn, you're out of here. Please continue Dr. Simon."

"As I was saying, I believe that Van suffers from manic depression and it has been my experience that people suffering from manic depression attempt suicide three times and are successful the third time."

"Great. Well, Evelyn, your favorite kid is fucked up."
She knew she shouldn't have said "fucked" but Dr. Simon
didn't seem to mind.

Van was discharged the following day and Taylor took
him home. She banned Evelyn from her house and Van was
relieved not to have to deal with his mother. Evelyn sent
Vita over to their house every day to spy. Vita ran
interference for her brother, telling her mother everything
was fine and relaying messages to Jayne and Maureen. By
this time, Boone was honorably discharged, living back at
home and holding down a full time job but for all the notice
Evelyn gave him, he could have still been in Japan.

JULY

A FRIDAY NIGHT

Thena decided to swing by Taylor's on her way home
from work. She hadn't been over since Van came home
from the hospital. Van was standing on the curb when she
came around the corner and pulled up in front of the house;
before she could turn off the car he opened up her car door,
grabbed her by the arm, yanked her out of her car and took
off.

"What the hell? Van, come back here," she yelled. So
she stood on the curb, in the same spot he'd tossed her and
waited. She kept looking up at the house, trying to figure
out what to say if Taylor saw her standing there. Twenty
minutes later he pulled up.

"You son-of-a bitch, you stole my car and my purse," she
said in a low tone because she didn't want Taylor to hear her.

"Borrowed," he said tossing her the car keys.

"I know where you went."

"You can't prove it."

"I've got a glass pack and it's loud. I counted the blocks
till the rumbling stopped."

"So what are you going to do? Are you going to tell
her?"

"No, I'm not going to tell her because then she will hate me. I'm waiting for her to find out for herself."

"Suit yourself."

"I'm pissed damn it. Don't you ever mess with my car again." It was her first car, a 1962 Chevy Impala hardtop sedan in mint condition. It looked gold but the title said the color was "Champagne" and she thought that was classy.

"You'll get over it," he winked at her and walked inside.

"You ass, don't you wink at me. Someday Taylor is going to find out you know. Your luck can't hold out forever," she whispered walking in the front door behind him.

OCTOBER

Van finally kept a job more than three months and Taylor got a job doing the books at The First Edition bar on Warren Avenue. It was the perfect job because she worked nights so when Van came home from work, she left and they didn't have to pay a babysitter. They were actually making money and able to buy a newer car. Things were finally looking up.

NOVEMBER
TUESDAY THE 4TH

"First Edition," Taylor answered the phone in the office. It was 10:00PM.

"Taylor, I came over and Van asked me to watch the kids while he went to the store for cigarettes and he ran into a tree on Whitlock. He wasn't hurt but the car had to be towed," Vita said.

"He ran my new car into a tree? Is he drunk or high?"

"All I know is he called from Chorty's and wants you to pick him up there on your way home from work."

"So the car gets towed and he can't ask the tow truck driver for a ride home?"

"That's all I know."

70

"How did he get to Chorty's?"

"I don't know, he walked I guess."

"And he couldn't walk home?"

"I don't know. I really don't know."

"I think you do know. Don't you ever get tired of covering for him?"

"I'm not covering for him.

Vita had the Van gene. She could lie, cheat and steal if it served her purpose without a twinge of guilt or remorse. Jill was the manager of the Women's Department and got Vita a job at K-Mart. After two weeks, Vita was fired for stealing. Jill was mortified but Vita was only upset because she got caught.

"Are the kids asleep? Taylor sighed."

"Yes."

"I'll be home in a couple hours with your useless brother."

FRIDAY THE 7TH

The phone rang.

"Mrs. Thomas, I am calling from AAA about the accident the other night. Can you describe to me in detail how the accident happened?" the insurance adjuster asked.

"I don't know how it happened, I wasn't there," Taylor replied.

"The police report says a woman was driving the car, I assumed it was you. A relative perhaps?" He hated these kinds of calls because it was always the worst case scenario. He always added "a relative perhaps" to try to lessen the impact of his call because he and the wife both knew her old man was fooling around.

"Well it wasn't me and it wasn't a relative either."

"I'm sorry, Mrs. Thomas. Please have your husband call me."

Taylor was sitting on the couch, drinking Pepsi and smoking a cigarette when Van got home from work.

"The insurance adjuster called, he wants to talk to you about who was driving the car."

"I was driving," Van said.

"Don't lie to me. I know when you're lying that's why I try not to ask you any questions. Who was driving the damn car?"

"Gloria Alexander."

"She's not even old enough to have a driver's license. She's jail bait. How stupid are you? I get that you're not afraid of me but I thought you'd be afraid of getting charged with statutory rape."

"I don't feel like fighting with you."

"I don't care what you feel like you prick."

Van went into their bedroom and slammed the door. He didn't come out until Taylor left for work. There really wasn't any way to get out of this one except silence.

Taylor stopped by Vince's Club on her way to work to talk to Mary Alexander, Gloria's mother, and the owner of the bar.

"Did you know Gloria smacked a tree with my car?" Taylor asked.

"How did she get your car?" Mary asked.

"She was with my old man."

"What was she doing with your old man?"

"You tell me, you're her mother."

"She's 14. She's a handful. I can't keep track of her all the time."

"From what I hear, you don't keep track of her at all."

"No need to get insulting. You've got insurance, why don't you so use it. I'll tell her not to drive your car again."

"Thanks for nothing," Taylor stormed out of the bar mad at herself for ignoring Van's affairs for so long, mad at Van, mad at Tim for covering for Van, mad at Vita for lying for Van, mad at the world. She knew she wasn't going to be able to ignore Van's affairs much longer.

FRIDAY THE 15TH

This is bad and low even for me but it feels so good, Van thought laying on his back watching Gloria move up and down on his manhood. You couldn't even classify it as an attack of conscience because it was so fleeting. She was naked, she was jail bait, she had a magnificent body and she knew how to use it. His hands were cupping her breasts, he could go to jail but it was more likely this was one more reason that he would go to hell.

Taylor came home from work early because she had a migraine. She stood in her bedroom doorway and watched Van and Gloria fucking in her bed. She didn't yell because she didn't want to wake up her kids. Then Van looked over and right into Taylor's eyes.

"What the hell is wrong with you? Your kids are sleeping in the next room."

Gloria rolled off Van and clutched the sheet to her chest with both hands.

"You're caught, little girl," Taylor said picking Gloria's clothes up off of the bedroom floor, carrying them through the living room and throwing them out the front lawn.

Gloria turned to Van, "What am I going to do?"

"I'd run if I were you," Van replied.

And run she did, right past Taylor and out the front door. Naked, with her dyed black ratted hair and heavy make-up, she did look a lot older than 14.

"Don't you ever bring one of your sluts into my house again. Do you hear me?"

"I hear you," he replied grabbing his pack of Camels off the nightstand.

"I'm going to lay down on the couch because I just can't deal with you right now. Don't touch me, don't talk to me, don't even look my way."

He laid in bed, staring at the ceiling. He lit a cigarette and in his own perverse way, he was relieved he'd finally been caught.

73

The next day Taylor stripped the sheets from the bed, took them out into the alley, threw them in a garbage can and burned them. Then she went back up to Vince's Club to talk to Mary, "Your daughter went from driving my car to fucking my old man."

"I thought she quit doing that stuff," Mary replied.

She looked at Mary, took out a cigarette and tapped it on the bar, in the time it took her to light it and take a drag, she decided she was tired of fighting a battle she knew she couldn't win, turned around and left.

DECEMBER

After the incident with Gloria, Van decided he would chill for a while but that he was definitely through with jail bait. He wanted to try to be the husband and father he swore to himself he would be when he was in the Brig. He infrequently saw Maureen and Jayne because they both had boyfriends but if the urge and opportunity presented itself, they got it on.

Taylor was relieved their lives had finally settled down but she wasn't about to be lulled into a false sense of security. She was far too cynical for that so for the time being she would just try to relax and when he went back to his evil ways, she'd decide what to do then. She'd given up on moving back to California a long time ago or ever seeing the Pacific Ocean again. She knew that Van didn't get that when Judge Alcini said "to love and honor", that meant don't screw around.

CHAPTER ELEVEN

1970

It was a good year. Van had a steady job and Taylor was still working at the First Edition. The kids were doing well. Taylor was letting her guard down a little but she remained cautiously optimistic. Big Joe had a lady friend and Lorraine had a good job in Dearborn close to the house. That was a good thing because Lorraine refused to drive on freeways. If she needed to go anywhere that involved an expressway, Thena or Taylor drove her. However, Lorraine and Tim were still going together and while Taylor never saw it, she heard when Tim was drunk, he was knocking Lor around. Hadn't Lor learned anything at all from her life? She thought about telling Aunt Chi Chi but until she was sure it was more than a rumor, she'd keep her eyes and ears open and her mouth shut.

AUGUST

Tim finally went too far. He beat Lor so badly that she ended up in the hospital. Taylor and Van were in her hospital room when Tim stumbled into the room.

"What the hell's wrong with you?" Van asked.

A short little nurse barely 5 feet tall walked into the Lorraine's room behind Tim. She grabbed Tim by the front of his shirt, spun him around and pinned him to the wall.

"You sorry excuse for man. You are the reason she is in here. I don't want to see you in this room again and if I do, I will call the police."

"I am the police," he slurred.

"Why doesn't that surprise me? If you come back in here again, you won't be "the police" for long. I promise you that. Now get out of here and don't come back." She released her hold on him and shoved him out the door.

Van followed him out into the hallway. "You really fucked up. You don't hit a woman and Jesus Christ, she's half your size."

"No, you don't hit them, you just fuck them. Now you know why I never wanted a girlfriend. Catch you on the green." He got on the elevator and was gone.

Lorraine never spoke to Tim again. Van and Tim's increasingly tenuous friendship was all but over and Taylor wondered if her and Lorraine would ever be happy. Big Joe blamed himself and Carlos loaded his rifle and sat in his mother's dinning room while Mama and Chi Chi told him they would like nothing better than to have Carlos kill Tim but they didn't want him going to prison over a such a worthless man. They convinced him that the best thing the family could do was to help Lorraine get on with her life, and they did.

SEPTEMBER
THAT'S ONE SMART CHICKEN

Over the years Chauncey graduated from eating live mice to live rats to live chickens. Van went to the poultry store on Warren Avenue to buy a live chicken for Chauncey's dinner like he'd done many Saturdays before but the chicken he brought home this time was no ordinary chicken. This

76

was Super Chicken. Unlike all the other chickens that died in the coils of the boa constrictor, this chicken made friends with the snake. As soon as Van dropped the chicken into Chauncey's aquarium and before Chauncey could strike, Super Chicken perched on his back, stared straight into his eyes, and there she stayed and there he laid. Instead of watching Chauncey digesting his prey, day after day Boone, Mike Summerville and Ray Hammond came over and watched the Mexican Standoff between Chauncey and Super Chicken and day after day they both maintained their motionless positions. Van knew that Chauncey was really hungry when he dropped the chicken into the aquarium so he didn't want to put his hand in the aquarium and pull Super Chicken out. It took 14 days for Super Chicken to go to the big chicken coop in the sky, still sitting upright on Chauncey's back and Chauncey still wouldn't eat the chicken. That night Chauncey joined Super Chicken.

"That was one hell of a smart chicken," Van said.

"I bring him home on a plane in a diaper bag and he gets taken out by a chicken," Taylor said.

OCTOBER
A FRIDAY NIGHT

Van, Boone, Mike and Ray stopped at Stromboli's for a late night pizza.

"Hi, Boone, long time no see," their waitress said.

"Sue Castanetti," Boone replied.

"Little Sue Castanetti?" Mike asked.

"I'll be dammed. I haven't seen you since junior high school," Ray said.

She turned to Van and said, "I don't think we've met."

"That's because he skipped school more than he went," Mike quipped.

"That's my brother Van."

"Ah, Van Thomas, my but aren't you the legend. You and those big, blue eyes. Didn't you go with Taylor Ginetti once upon a time?"

"You seem to know a lot about me, how do I get to know you?"

"Why don't you order and we can figure that out later."

"Cheese, two pepperoni pizzas and four PBRs."

"One pie and four Pabst coming up."

"She's not bad," Van said.

"Down boy," Boone said.

"She likes me."

"You think every woman likes you. Jesus, eat your pizza and drink your beer," Mike said.

"You boys need anything else?" Sue asked.

"No, we're good," Van answered.

"I bet you are," she winked at him and laid their bill on the table.

"Christ, she wrote her phone number on the bill," Boone said.

"I'll take that," Van said, grabbing it out of Boone's hand.

"Then you'll pay it too," Boone said and the three of them got up leaving Van to pay the check.

Van asked her out and she accepted. They were both married with three kids but they didn't care.

* * *

When Taylor discovered she was pregnant again, she couldn't believe it. She was on the pill but her doctor pretty much told her shit happens. Van was home less and less and this time he wasn't even trying to hide he had something going on the side. She knew she shouldn't sleep with him but she hated him and she loved him at the same time. She hated herself for not hating him enough. She got herself in this mess. She couldn't blame Van for this. This was all on her. She was tired and weary. She cried when she was alone and the kids were in bed, even Lorraine never saw her cry. She prided herself on being in control but she knew she was never in control and would never be in control until she got

78

rid of Van. Her life wasn't supposed to be like this. Other people had good marriages and nice homes like she had when her Mom was alive. Other people were dealt a full house and she wasn't even holding a pair of deuces.

* * *

This wasn't the first affair Sue had during her marriage but her husband Mark chose not to deal with her infidelities because he didn't want to lose his daughters. He was the male version of Taylor, taking care of his kids and pretending nothing was wrong.

DECEMBER

Taylor knew if she could just get through holidays, she could make the decision she had been putting off for years but Van always got what he wanted and Taylor was too tired to keep living this way. She finally arrived at the point where it took less energy to kick him out than to stay with him. The thought of enduring one more Christmas Eve at Evelyn's didn't thrill her but just knowing it was the last time she would ever step foot into that damn house gave her the strength to get through it. The drama at the Thomas house no longer thrilled her.

CHAPTER TWELVE

1971

JANUARY

Taylor applied for ADC and got it. She hated going on welfare but for the time being, it was the only way her and her kids could survive. If she kicked Van out, she could keep her part-time bookkeeping job at The First Edition and they would pay for her babysitter. With her plan in place, Taylor told Van they were through. The same week Sue Poole packed up her kids, the furniture and all of her worldly possessions and left her husband when he was at work and Van, Boone and Mike helped her move.

Van and Sue rented a house as "Mr. & Mrs. Thomas" on the other side of the Southfield Freeway, a couple miles from Taylor's house. Thena knew the house all too well, her older brother, Luke, rented the same tiny two bedroom bungalow in 1963 right after he got married. The layout was weird, one bathroom, a living room, kitchen and two bedrooms, one bedroom off of the living room and the other one was upstairs. The house sat on the back of the lot so there was a lot of front yard and no backyard.

"If that bitch used my name . . ." Taylor said.

"Don't get pissed yet," Thena interrupted. "I mean, of course you are pissed but before you hit the maximum pissed let me check it out."

"And how are you going to do that?"

"I'll call Luke. He's like my Dad, he never throws anything out. I bet he still has the Landlord's phone number." And she was right, he did.

"Hello, my name is Mrs. McGuire and I am calling from State Farm Insurance Company to verify the address for a house on Grandview rented by a Mr. & Mrs. Van Thomas," Thena said.

"Van and Sue Thomas are renting the house at 1122 Grandview in Detroit," the Landlord confirmed. He was a nice man, they exchanged a few pleasantries and the deed was done.

"It was almost too easy. At least now we know she's not using your name," Thena laughed.

"Nothing is easy. You ought to know that by now," Taylor replied. "So now she's Sue Thomas."

* * *

While Taylor knew exactly what was going on in her marriage, Mark Poole didn't have a clue. All he knew is once again, his wife left him and this time she took everything but an old coffee pot. A couple days later Sue called Mark and gave him her address so he could see their kids. Van made sure he wasn't around when Mark picked up or dropped off the kids and Sue told her daughters, Kathleen, Eileen and Missy, not to tell Daddy about Van because he would get very mad.

THURSDAY NIGHT, JANUARY 21ST

Van couldn't make a clean break from Taylor because even with all of his fucking around, he still loved her so he bounced back and forth between both houses. Three weeks after Taylor told him to leave, he came walking into the house and sat in the chair in front of the T.V. and she was sitting in her usual spot on the couch.

"Isn't your honey going to miss you?"

"I thought I'd spend the night."

"You thought wrong. Van, I want you out of here for good."

"I don't want to leave you when you're pregnant."

"You've never been with me when I was pregnant, why should this time be any different?

"It just doesn't seem right, us actually splitting up."

"You have got to be kidding me. Nothing about this is right. When have you ever cared about 'right'? Who are you?"

"You know I've always loved you and I'll always love you."

"If I didn't know you better, I'd think you actually feel guilty but we both know guilt has never been one of your emotions. You just don't get it. I don't care if you love me. We have different ideas of what love is. We get along just fine until our feet hit the floor and that's not love."

She watched him get up and go into the bedroom to pack the rest of his clothes. When he was done, he came out of the bedroom with a duffle bag, walked over to the couch, bent down, kissed her on the forehead and he left.

Taylor sat there for a long time, staring out the front door. Lorraine pulled up with Sarah, Van and Vanessa and it occurred to her she was still more upset about losing her Mustang than she was about losing Van.

"What's wrong?" Lorraine asked.

"Van's gone," Taylor answered.

"It's about time. It's not like the kids are going to miss him. He was never here."

"No more snakes, no more Evelyn."

"No more asshole."

"Asshole," Vanessa repeated.

"That will look good in her baby book, called Daddy asshole," Taylor said.

* * *

FEBRUARY

Mike Summerville asked Taylor if he and his girlfriend, Amy, could move in with her until they got a place of their own. Amy was five months pregnant with their first kid. Taylor didn't know Amy that well but Mike was easy going and made her laugh so she figured what the hell.

"We want to get a place before the baby is born," Mike said.

"Stay as long as you need to," Taylor said.

"You think Van will care?"

"This isn't Van's house, its mine."

TUESDAY, APRIL 20TH

"Hi, it's me. I had a boy. I'm fine. He's fine, everything's fine," Taylor told Thena.

"I'll be up to see you this afternoon.

"Evelyn and Van just left."

'Un fuckin' believable. You told them not to come."

"They never listened to me before so why should they now. I wouldn't let them hold him. I told the nurses to keep the baby in the Nursery."

"Did you name him yet?"

"Not yet, he's still Baby Boy Thomas."

"We can talk about names when I get there. Do you want me to bring you anything."

"An ice cold bottle of Pepsi. The food is cold here and the pop is warm."

"You got it. See you later."

"I don't know how she is going to do it, Matt. I can't imagine taking care of four kids all by myself," Thena told her 11 month old son.

* * *

Providence Hospital had strictly enforced rules. Only two visitors per patient at a time and you had to get pass at the Information Desk in order to get to the elevator. Both of Taylor's visitor's passes were out so Thena sat on a bench in front of the elevators reading a magazine and waiting for what she thought would be Big Joe and Lorraine but then the elevator doors opened and out walked Boone with Jayne Fitzpatrick. She watched them from behind the magazine until they walked out the lobby's revolving door.

"What the hell. I can't believe what I just saw," Thena said setting a pot of violets, Taylor's favorite flowers, on the windowsill and handing Taylor the Pepsi.

"They brought me flowers, wasn't that nice of them?" Taylor said sarcastically pointing to the wastebasket. "They're dating."

"You've got to be kidding me. They're dating? Don 't they know you know about her and Van?"

"They don't care what I know, they never have."

"So now Boone's into sloppy seconds?"

"Boone will always be second because he doesn't know how to be first."

"So is Van still fucking her?"

"She's not knocked up, so I guess not," Taylor laughed. "This Pepsi tastes good."

"I'm glad you have a sense of humor about this."

"What else am I going to do? Oh woe is me?"

"He was a first class dick bringing her up here."

"He's a Thomas so what's new? Three of them in one day is way too many for me."

"Here's your robe and slippers. I want to see the baby."

"First let me finish my Pepsi."

They walked down the hall to the Nursery and stood there looking into the Nursery window at all the babies.

"I could pick him out without looking at his name tag," Thena said.

"I know," Taylor whispered.

"What's wrong?"

"I have to name him before I can bring him home and I can't think of a name."

"Oh hell no, I know what you're thinking and don't you dare name that innocent little baby Van."

"He looks like Van."

"They all look like Van."

"I know but I can't think of another name and I just want to get out of here. It's just a name."

SUNDAY, MAY 9TH

It was 6:00 PM and Mark Poole was an hour early dropping his kids off at what he thought was his wife's rented house. He knocked on the door and she didn't answer.

"Sue, Sue I brought the kids home," he called out.

Still no answer.

Since her car was in the driveway, he figured she was home. He turned the front door knob and it opened.

"Sue," he called out again.

Again, no answer.

"You girls wait right here for Daddy. I'm going to check upstairs. Maybe Mommy is taking a nap."

Sue and Van were too involved in their carnal pursuit to hear Mark calling and by the time they realized he was standing next to the bed, it was too late. Sue jumped up and grabbed for her robe, it was then that he got a good look at her previously concealed pregnant belly. Since she hadn't slept with him in over a year, he knew the baby wasn't his. Now, everybody will tell you that Mark Poole was a nice guy. When Sue got pregnant the third time his brother, Ben, told him she was screwing around and the kid wasn't his and even though he knew in his heart Missy wasn't his, he loved her because he figured it wasn't the kid's fault. But even nice guys have a breaking point and Mark didn't say a word, he just started swinging and beating the shit out of Van.

"Stop, Mark, stop, please stop," Sue cried.

Van laid there and let Mark beat him because he was afraid if he didn't, Mark would go for Sue.

"GET OUT," Mark yelled. "I want to talk to my loving wife. Don't worry, I'm not going to hit her. Not that I don't want to hit her, but I won't."

Van looked over at Sue and she nodded for him to go. His eyes were swelling shut, he could feel the blood running out of his nose onto the top of his split lip, he ran his tongue over his teeth and they were all there. He sat on the side of the bed for a minute, trying to remember where he put his clothes. He was in shock. *So this is what it feels like to get the shit kicked out of you,* he thought. He grabbed his jeans and t-shirt off the floor, got dressed and remembered his shoes were in the living room. He walked downstairs and sat on the couch because he wasn't steady enough to stand up and put on his shoes.

"Did my Daddy do that?" Six year old Kathleen asked pointing at Van's face.

"No, your Daddy didn't do this. I fell. I want you girls to go into your room and shut your door until Mommy says you can come out."

"We didn't tell," five year old Eileen cried out.

"I know you didn't tell besides there isn't anything to tell now is there?"

"No, there isn't anything to tell," Kathleen answered.

"Listen to me, this isn't your fault. Kathleen, take Eileen and Missy and go wait in your room. Go on now; everything is going to be okay."

He couldn't avoid 3 year old Missy's eyes and it unnerved him. That look would haunt him for the rest of his life. It was like she knew nothing would ever be okay again.

The thought crossed his mind that Mark had guys waiting outside to jump him. He slowly opened the front door, nobody there and before he closed the door he heard Mark yell, "You're nothing but a whore. I'm getting a divorce and taking the girls."

About the only thing that mattered to Van were his good looks and his flawless face was battered, bloody and bruised. He walked into the Warrendale and sat down at the bar next to Mike, Ray and Boone. Buzz set him up with a double shot straight up and he scored two Vicodin off of Boone.

"Your face looks like it went through a meat grinder What the hell happened to you?" Boone asked taking a swallow of beer.

Sullivan and Kowalski put down their pool sticks, grabbed their longnecks and sat down at the bar. Some of the guys thought this day had been a long time coming but kept it to themselves. Most of the girls thought Mark should have beaten his bitch wife too, again keeping it to themselves. Word spread fast and Van knew he had an additional problem; he had to tell Taylor that Sue was pregnant before she heard it from somebody else. And if Lorraine found out before Taylor, Jesus he shuttered to think about it.

Van called Taylor from the bar at midnight

"You heard?" Van asked.

"Mike told me," she answered.

"Can I come home and spend the night?"

"That's an interesting choice of words."

"Can I?"

"Yes." Taylor hung up the phone and looked at the 8x10 color portrait of Van still sitting on her dresser. It was taken in San Diego. He was in his dress whites with a ship in the background. She liked the picture and didn't see any reason to remove it, removing him was enough. About 20 minutes later Van called again.

"Sue came up to the bar. She doesn't want me to see you so I'm going home with her," Van said.

"She's jealous of me? Maybe you better remind your girlfriend, I'm your wife," Taylor said and hung up the phone. Van had never lost a fight, let alone walked away from one with his face fucked up and she knew he couldn't, or more to the point, he wouldn't let it go.

MONDAY, MAY 10TH

It was 11:30AM and Taylor was standing in her kitchen, looking out the front window, talking to Thena on the telephone.

"Something's up, Van came over and got Mike and they weren't going to work."

"So they skipped work and went fishing," Thena said.

"No, because when I asked Van where they were going he said 'I'm going to kill him.' This is why I don't ask him questions."

"Those were his exact words?"

"Yes, and Ray and Boone went with them," Taylor said taking a drag off of her cigarette.

Mike cut through the alley, hopped the fence, ran through the backyard and in the side door with Ray right behind him. *Shotgun* by Jr. Walker and the All Stars was playing on the radio.

"Who is that?" Mike yelled.

"What's wrong with you? Who is who?" Taylor asked.

"On the phone, is that the cops?"

"It's Thena. Oh my God, he did it. He killed him."

"Hang up the phone."

"I heard that," Thena said.

"I'll call you back," Taylor hung up the phone and leaned against the sink.

"Is Van here?" Boone ran in the front door and grabbed the back of a chair at the kitchen table trying to catch his breath.

"No, Van's not here. Somebody tell me what happened?" Taylor demanded.

"Which way did he go?" Boone asked.

"For Faygo. Hell, I don't know which way I went. I wasn't keeping track of him," Mike said, standing by the side door. He was the only one that wasn't out of breath. Terror is a great motivator.

"Fuck. Oh God, I feel sick. "Mother fucker, mother fucker," Ray said shaking his head. He was over 6 feet tall and weighed close to 300 pounds. This was the first and only time Taylor had ever seen Ray scared.

Taylor handed Ray a cold Pepsi to steady his nerves. He was shaking so badly he sat down at the kitchen table and had to hold the bottle with both hands.

"Somebody tell me what happened," Taylor said her hands shaking as she lit another cigarette and handed it to Mike.

"We went over there and Mark Poole was there and Van held the shotgun on him and told him to leave," Ray said.

"He was leaving; he knew he was outnumbered and he didn't have a death wish," Mike said taking a drag off of his cigarette.

"Are you sure he's dead?" Taylor asked.

"Oh, he's dead," Boone said.

"Okay, okay, were the kids there?"

"They saw it."

"What the hell happened to those kids?"

"We carried them out of the house and put them on the sidewalk and told them to stay there till their Mom came out," Mike answered.

"Then we ran," Ray said.

"Fuckin' adults, you can't keep your messes to yourselves," Taylor said.

"IT ISN'T OUR MESS," Boone yelled.

"IT IS NOW," Taylor yelled back.

Vance and Vanessa were watching TV in Taylor's bedroom and baby Van was sleeping in his crib. She told them to stay put and shut the door. Thank God Sarah was in school because she never would have stayed in the bedroom.

"We have to call the cops," Boone said.

"No cops," Ray said.

"He's right. Think about it. It will look better for us," Mike said.

Boone picked up the phone. "Operator, I need to talk to Schaefer Station. Yes, it is an emergency. Hello, my name is Boone Thomas and I'm reporting a shooting."

"Just a minute," the cop said.

"The bastard put me on hold. I don't think he believes me."

The cop came back on the line, Boone listened for a couple minutes, gave the cop Taylor's address and hung up the phone.

"They know all about it. Sue Poole dropped a dime. They know our names and they're on their way."

"Did he say if the kids are okay?" Ray asked.

"After what they saw, those kids will never be okay," Taylor said.

Van ran in Ted Cooper's side door and Minnie was sitting at her kitchen table smoking a cigarette and drinking a cup of coffee. His face was white as a ghost and his body was splattered with blood.

"Is that your blood?" Minnie asked.

"No."

"Don't tell me what you did, I don't want to know."

Taylor's phone rang.

"Don't answer it," Ray said.

"Why? The cops know where you are," Taylor said.

"I shot him," Van said.

"I know."

"Come and get me."

Taylor drove down Paul to Longacre and pulled into Ted's driveway. Van ran out the side door and ducked into the car.

"What the hell did you do?" Taylor asked.

"You don't need to know what happened. It's better for you that way."

They drove up Whitlock and looked down Memorial at the cops surrounding Evelyn's house.

"Evelyn is really going to be pissed," Van said.

"I'm pretty sure that cops surrounding her house aren't why she is going to be pissed."

Taylor backed into her driveway and Van slid out of the car and ran in the side door. She followed him into the house and Mike, Boone and Ray were still in the kitchen where she left them.

"Cops are all over the house. Did you call Mom?" Van asked Boone.

"Hell no," Boone answered in an *are you our of your mind* tone.

Van went into the bathroom, turned on the hot water and grabbed the soap to wash off the blood. He really wanted to take a shower but he knew the cops would be pulling up any minute and he didn't want them to come into the house to get him. He watched Mark Poole's blood mingled with the water fill the sink and he started gagging. He never would get used to killing. Even in Nam, he dry heaved. He changed into the clean t-shirt and jeans he kept stashed in the bottom of the linen closet, came out, sat down on the couch and waited.

"Just so you don't think you pulled one over on me, I knew your clothes were hidden there," Taylor said.

Boone and Ray walked into the living room and sat down in the chairs. The sound of Zippo lighter lids slapping open and shut and nervous foot tapping replaced conversation.

"It won't be long before the cops get here," Van said.

As soon as Van finished his sentence, they heard sirens.

"I should have listened to Evelyn. She begged me not to go with you. She said you looked crazy," Boone said.

What do you know, Evelyn was worried about Boone, Taylor thought, but that in itself was terrifying if Evelyn thought Van looked crazy.

Taylor was on autopilot then she noticed Mike wasn't there.

"Where's Mike?"

"I'm here. Cops here yet?" Mike asked looking around the kitchen wall.

"No, where did you go?" Taylor asked.

"Downstairs, I put on a clean shirt. I don't know when I'll get a clean shirt again.

Tell Amy when she gets home. I don't want to call her at work because there's nothing she can do. When I find out how much bail is, I'll call her. But call my brother so he can tell my Mom before somebody else tells her."

"You guys are sure he's dead? I mean did you take his pulse? Maybe he's not dead," Taylor said.

"He instantly assumed room temperature," Ray said.

"Damn it, Taylor. I know dead when I see it," Van added.

Four cop cars pulled up and Van, Boone, Ray and Mike walked out onto the front porch and down the sidewalk. Taylor looked at her bedroom door, making sure it was still shut. She watched the cops slap the cuffs on their wrists.

"Why did they come here?" the cop that cuffed Van called to Taylor.

Taylor stepped out onto the front porch and she had a feeling he already knew the answer.

"She's my wife," Van answered.

"What a mess," the cop said pushing Van's head down and shoving him in the backseat of his squad car. Ray, Boone and Mike were pushed individually into the back seats of the other three squad cars.

Taylor watched them pull away. She was glad they didn't turn their sirens back on. Mike gave her a nod, Ray was slumped down, Van and Boone stared straight ahead.

Taylor went back into the house, opened her bedroom door and told the kids they could come out and called Thena.

"Is it on the news yet? I'm afraid to turn on the TV," Taylor asked.

"Shooting on Grandview, details at 6:00PM. It's not on TV yet but it's on the radio and they're calling it a love triangle."

"So it's a love triangle. Guess I don't count."

"Be glad they don't know about you yet."

"I have to go over there. I have to see it."

"There? You mean there, there, the house? Not a good idea. Very, very bad idea."

"You want to go with me? Lorraine can watch Matthew."

"You're serious. No I don't want to go with you and Lorraine's at work. Oh don't tell me you're calling her to come home."

"First I'm calling Lorraine and then Connie, she'll go with me."

"You're really going aren't you?" Why, why in the hell do you have to go over there? He's dead. You know he's dead. They all told you he's dead. The cops arrested them. He's dead."

"I have to see it."

"And what if he's still there? You want to look at a fresh dead body? You won't even go to the funeral home."

"I'm going, even if I have to go alone. I have to."

"You do not have to but I know you are going to. It's a crime scene for God sakes. The cops are going to be there. What makes you think you can get inside?"

"Then I'll ask questions and find out what I want to know."

"What do you want to know? He's dead. That's all they know right now. And I know you're thinking *blah blah* so I'll shut up and if you need bail, call me and watch it will you."

Lorraine reluctantly came home from work.

"And what if you get arrested?" Lorraine asked.

"Thena's going to throw bail."

"You're crazy."

"Like I haven't heard that before and don't tell Dad. I'll be back before Sarah gets home from school."

THE HOUSE ON GRANDVILLE

A cop was posted outside the front door and the Wayne County Coroner's wagon was backed into the driveway behind Van's car. It was actually a cargo van but for some unknown reason, everybody called it a "wagon".

Taylor parked in front of the house and they got out of the car and stood on the sidewalk.

"What's the plan? What are you going to tell the cops?" Connie asked.

"I want to go inside, I'm his wife."

"And you think that's going to work?"

"There's only one way to find out," she said walking up to the uniformed cop stationed at the front door.

"If you think you can handle it, go ahead," he said.

"If we can't, we will be right back out," Taylor said opening the screen door and stepping into the living room. The first thing they saw was blood splattered on the yellow shag carpet turning sections of it a rusty looking orange.

"Jesus, I've never seen so much blood," Connie said, looking for a clean patch of carpet to stand on.

"Neither have I," Taylor said carefully pushing the bloody curtain back from the window exposing Mark's right ear and a chunk of brain lying on top of the blood soaked window sill.

"Holy shit," Connie gagged and backed away, paying careful attention not to step in any blood.

"He blew his head off. They didn't tell me that," Taylor said fighting back the vomit creeping up her throat.

"I bet there's a lot they didn't tell you."

Taylor walked out of the house just as the morgue wagon pulled out of the driveway and she made the sign of the cross.

"And I didn't think things could get any worse."

* * *

94

"Mommy, Mommy, is my Daddy dead," Sarah cried running in the front door and into her mother's arms. "Raydean's Mommy came to school and Raydean said my Daddy's dead and her Daddy's in jail."

"You should have gone to school and picked her up."

"Ok Loraine, I didn't think she'd find out. I forgot about Raydean. Ray must have called Deanna for bail."

"Hello, didn't you think Deanna would see the cop cars? She lives down the street."

"No, Lorraine, I didn't think. Okay, I didn't think.

Sarah, Daddy's not dead. Raydean is right, her Daddy is in jail. So is your Daddy, Uncle Boone and Uncle Mike."

"Did they do something bad?"

"Daddy did something bad and they were there when he did it."

"Daddy kilt somebody and they took him to jail," Vance piped up.

"Shot him dead," Vanessa added.

So much for closing the bedroom door.

* * *

Thena called Taylor at 8:00PM.

"So, did you go?"

"You know I did. Connie almost threw up. It was pretty bad."

"And what about you?"

"When I saw the blood on the floor, I thought I could handle it. Then I saw the blood on the curtain and I pulled it back and his ear and part of his brain was on the windowsill. That was pretty bad. That's when Connie ran out."

"Oh my God, how could they miss that? How could they leave that laying there?"

"The yellow ribbon is still up so maybe they are coming back to take pictures or something. I don't know. He was reaching for the door, he thought he was safe and then the gun went off. He will always be reaching for the door."

"I still can't believe they let you in."

95

"After Connie went outside, I went upstairs and looked around the happy couple's bedroom."

"You what?"

"I had to know if Mark Poole really did go there looking for a fight."

"Of course you did and how in the hell can you tell that from looking at their bedroom?"

"It just came to me. I opened up the closet door and dresser drawers. That bitch's clothes are hanging in the closet and his are hidden in the dresser drawers."

"So what does that prove? I don't get it."

"Think about it. It's not obvious that Van lives here. There is nothing out in the open in that bedroom that is Van's. Mark Poole didn't know she was shacking up with Van. He really did just walk in on them."

"So?"

"So he didn't go there to ambush them. He didn't expect to walk in on them. What guy wouldn't react like he did to seeing his wife naked in bed fucking another guy?"

"Holy Mother of God. It was premeditated. I can't believe that those guys knew Van was going to kill him."

"He had a shotgun so maybe they just thought he was going to shoot him," Taylor said sarcastically. "You know what, we'll never know because they will never tell. They will take whatever really happened in that house to their graves."

* * *

Taylor visited Van in Wayne County Jail. Boone, Ray and Mike made bail but so far no bail was set for Van. He was the only white guy in there. Only relatives could visit and word on the street was Sue Poole was more upset about not being able to visit Van than she was about her dead husband.

"So she's pregnant," Taylor said.

"You found out," Van said.

"Yes, I found out. And it's yours?"

96

"Yes. I was going to tell you the night I called from the bar. I didn't want you to find out from somebody else."

"Well guess what, I did. The front page of the Warrendale Courier says you were a friend of Mrs. Poole's. You're some friend."

"I know, Evelyn told me."

"Mark Poole didn't deserve to die. What the hell is wrong with you?"

"Nam, drugs, booze, everything. Hell, Taylor, you and the kids are the only good things in my life and I know that but I'm long past being able to be your husband or their father."

"You're right but lucky you, you'll always be Evelyn's son."

"When I went in the Navy, I was going to be somebody."

"You shot that dream all to hell so deal with it. For once in your life, deal with what you did."

Taylor looked at the red rose tattoo with her name written on a ribbon below it on his arm, "I told you not to put my name on that tattoo but then I told you to quit fucking around and you didn't listen to me about that either."

* * *

Van spent two weeks in jail before his bail was set. Bob and Evelyn put up their house as security for his bond. He was released to Taylor and they had an appointment with his court appointed attorney, Maxwell Howard, the same day.

"Did you kill Mr. Poole?" Howard asked.

"Yes," Van answered and then he started to explain.

"Stop, I don't want to hear it. You need to keep out of trouble, move back in with your wife and you won't do any more time."

"Move back in with me? Why can't he live with his mother?"

"It's appearances that are going to keep him out of jail, it's sure not the facts so if his wife can forgive him, the Judge may be inclined to also. As it stands now, I am going to have to pull a rabbit out of my hat and you are my rabbit."

"What about a jury trial?" Van asked.

"The Judge we pulled is a man. We request a jury trial and we don't know how many women we will get. Take my advice, you don't want even one woman deciding your fate."

They walked outside and got in Taylor's car.

"So I'm stuck with you again," Taylor said.

"I promise no trouble. I will stay straight and no fooling around," Van said.

"You play that tune like an old record. You can move back in but as soon as soon as that bitch's kid is born, you're out of the house and out of my life."

TUESDAY, JULY 13TH

It was like a scene out of a 1940's B movie, the wife and the mistress standing in the hallway across from each other waiting for the murder trial of their husband and lover to begin. They were wearing the same dress they bought the day before but in different colors, Taylor's was black and Sue's was brown and, of course, everybody noticed. Sue also wore a baggy white sweater to hide her ever growing belly.

Both the Thomas and Poole families were giving Taylor dirty looks and made her feel like she was the one that pulled the trigger. How did she become the enemy? Was it because Evelyn blamed her for Van's downfall? Did the Poole family hate her because she was Van's wife? Why didn't they see that she was the female counterpart of Mark but she had been left breathing to deal with it all? Boone hadn't talked to her since the day of the murder and he never spoke to her again.

Taylor and Connie stayed in the hallway smoking a cigarette while the Thomas and Poole families walked into and sat on opposite sides of the courtroom. They didn't see Boone, Mike or Ray and figured they were off in a room somewhere waiting to testify. Mike still lived at Taylor's

98

house and they left for Court at the same time so she knew he was there somewhere. They walked into the courtroom and sat in the last row on the Poole side behind a detective holding 8 x 10 glossies of the crime scene. Taylor looked over the detective's shoulder at the pictures of Mark Poole's body lying on the floor covered with blood; the right side of his head was gone. Tears rolled down her cheeks, she sat back and waited for the trial to begin.

The Judge had black hair and wore wire rim glasses. It was difficult to figure out his age, sitting behind that big bench and wearing the black robe. It was even harder to figure him out because his expression never changed. He never smiled and he never frowned, he just listened and he took notes.

After opening arguments, testimony began and the Prosecutor called Boone's name.

"Do you swear that the testimony you are about to give is the truth, the whole truth and nothing but the truth, so help you God?" the Deputy asked.

"I do," Boone answered, putting down his right hand and sitting in the witness box on the left side of the Judge's bench.

"Like he is going to tell the truth," Connie whispered.

"State your name for the record," the Prosecutor said.

"Boone Victor Thomas."

"How are your related to the Defendant?"

"He's my older brother."

After the Prosecutor asked Boone who else was at the house and why they went to the house, he asked the $64,000 question, the question everybody in the room was waiting to hear.

"Please explain in your own words what happened that day."

"Van, my brother, put the barrel of the gun on the back of Mark Poole's head and told him to leave and it went off."

"By it went off, you mean Van Thomas, your brother, pulled the trigger?"

"No, that's not what I mean. I mean the gun went off. I didn't see him pull the trigger."

I call Michael Anthony Summerville to the stand.

"Van nudged Mark Poole with the barrel of the gun on the back of his head and told him to leave and it went off."

"So Van Thomas placed the barrel of the shotgun on the back of Mark Poole's head, pushed him with it, fired the weapon and blew off the right side of Mark Poole's head, severing his ear and dislodging a portion of his brain," the Prosecutor said.

"I didn't see him pull the trigger."

"I call Raymond Paul Hammond to the stand."

Ray pretty much set the scene the same way and said, "I didn't see him pull the trigger."

When Court adjourned, Connie and Taylor decided to go around the block to Maria's Italian Restaurant for lunch.

"Oh God, look at what just walked in," Taylor said.

Connie looked toward the door and watched the entire Thomas family walk in with Van and Sue.

"Those people are morally corrupt. You let him move back in with you to help save his ass and they have that bitch with them?" Connie said.

"I feel sick," Taylor said.

"We're going to finish eating. I am not giving them the satisfaction of driving us out of here. Order a Vernors, that will help settle your stomach."

Taylor ate as much as she safely felt she could swallow and drank two glasses of Vernors. Connie threw a couple packets of crackers into her purse, just in case Taylor needed them, and they walked over to the register to pay their bill. Van walked over to Taylor and whispered in her ear, "Don't worry. It's going to be okay."

Taylor didn't look at him and she didn't speak to him. Connie watched him walk back to the table and if looks could kill, he'd be deader that poor Mark Poole.

The trial reconvened and Wayne County's ballistics expert testified that the safety was not faulty and for the gun to discharge, the trigger had to have been pulled. Maxwell Howard tried hard but he couldn't shake his testimony. The prosecution rested and Court was over for the day.

When Van came home, Taylor was waiting for him. "Grab your clothes, get out and don't come back. I don't care where you go or what you do. How did I end up the bad one? You and that bitch are guilty, not me. Once again, everybody is blaming me; you get off and I get screwed."

"I haven't gotten off and nobody blames you. Lorraine and Big Joe hate me; the Summervilles and the Hammonds blame me; Deanna and Amy hate me."

"But you deserve it. Your family and the Pooles look at me like I should be dead and I don't deserve that."

"You don't deserve that."

"Just get out."

"Will you be in Court tomorrow?"

"I'll be there. I don't want to be, but I will."

WEDNESDAY, JULY 14TH

Court resumed and it was Maxwell Howard's turn.

"Mr. Thomas, please tell us in your own words what happened."

"Sue called me. . ."

"When you say Sue, you are referring to Sue Poole?"

"Yes, she said Mark Poole was at the house and she was afraid."

"Objection Your Honor, hearsay and calls for speculation," the Prosecutor said.

"Sustained," the Judge ruled.

"Let me rephrase. Van, why were you at the house?"

"I was worried about Sue."

"Why were you worried?"

"Because he, Mark, beat me up the night before."

"Is it safe for me to say that you were angry."

"Yes."

"Your Honor, at this time I would like to introduce Defendant's Exhibit 1 into evidence, the Lease for the house on Grandville with Van Thomas' signature on it."

"Your Honor, we stipulate that Mr. Thomas' name is on the Lease," the Prosecutor said.

"Thank you. Van, did you go there with the intention of killing Mark Poole?"

"No."

"Then why did take a gun?"

"To scare him. The gun just went off."

The Prosecutor cross-examined Van but he couldn't shake his testimony. Neither side chose to put Sue Poole on the witness stand. A pregnant by the accused, non grieving widow of the victim wouldn't do anybody any good.

Maxwell Howard hoped his Closing Arguments would be the rabbit but even he knew the best he could hope for was to keep Van out of prison with minimum jail time.

"Your Honor, you heard Van Thomas tell us in his own words what happened. You heard the testimony of the other three gentlemen that were present when the unfortunate death of Mr. Poole occurred and despite the ballistics expert's testimony, nobody saw my client pull the trigger."

Taylor and Connie left the courtroom the minute the Judge left the bench and walked down four flights of stairs to the street; they didn't feel like riding the elevator.

Van called that night and Taylor told him to stay away. Sarah asked where Daddy was but Vance and Vanessa didn't seem to notice he was gone, to them it had become a way of life and Baby Van, he didn't even know who Van was.

THURSDAY, JULY 15TH

"After weighing the testimony and facts placed before this Court, I am ready to render my decision. Will the Defendant please rise."

Van's attorney tapped him on the shoulder and they both stood up.

"Mr. Thomas, I find the case that the Prosecutor presented to this Court to be factual and no matter what the circumstances, whether you pulled the trigger or didn't pull the trigger, a man is dead. However, because you were beaten rather severely by Mr. Poole, I find there to be mitigating circumstances. So, instead of finding you guilty of murder in the first degree, I find you guilty of manslaughter. You are ordered to pay restitution to Mr. & Mrs. Poole for their son's funeral expenses and I sentence you to time served and five years supervised probation."

The Poole side of the courtroom was in shock; the Thomas side of the courtroom was in awe; Maxwell Howard had indeed pulled a rabbit out of his hat.

The Judge banged his gavel and as quick as that, the trial was over.

Once again Connie and Taylor were the first ones out of the courtroom but this time they made the mistake of waiting for the elevator.

"I don't believe it. I just don't believe it," Connie said.

"He got away with it," Taylor said in tortured disbelief. "He killed him, he told me he was going to kill him and he walks away." She didn't know if she was relieved because, after all, he was the father of her kids or stunned because this was just one more terrible thing Evelyn's little boy got away with.

"You better kick him out for good now."

"When the kid is born, he is gone."

They were on elevator waiting for the doors to close when a male friend of Mark Poole's stepped in front of the elevator doors and spit in Taylor's face.

"WHAT THE HELL IS WRONG WITH YOU?" Connie yelled as the doors slid shut.

"Am I just as bad as Van? I pretended I didn't know about his affairs," Taylor whispered, she couldn't hold back the tears any more.

"No, don't even think like that. Mark Poole pretended that he didn't know about her affairs too," Connie said taking a tissue from her pocket and wiping the spit off Taylor's cheek. "But you can't be around those people anymore because they don't get it and this whole sordid mess will never end. I'm telling you the Pooles will never let this go but that guy was not a Poole and he didn't have any business doing what he did. He probably didn't have the balls to spit on Van so he spit on you."

A week after the trial, Van got his first telegram signed *"Mark Poole"*. Through the years, he would get them on the anniversary of Mark Poole's murder, on Mark Poole's birthday and on Christmas and random times throughout the year. Wherever he was, whatever he was doing, the telegrams found him and they always said the same thing, "I'm waiting for you".

WEDNESDAY, SEPTEMBER 22ND

After the trial, Van rarely went to see Sue and if she wasn't knocked up and for the fact that he killed her husband, he would have moved on by now. Then late one night when Van and Taylor were sleeping the phone rang and Taylor answered it.

"Is Van there?"

"Who wants to know?"

"Angelina, Sue's sister."

Taylor yelled to Van but he wouldn't get up so she stretched the telephone cord to the bedroom, shook him awake and handed him the phone.

"Uh huh, uh huh," was all he said and he handed the phone back to Taylor, she walked back into the kitchen and hung it up.

"She's having the kid isn't she," Taylor said and Van didn't move. "Get up and go."

He still didn't move.

She threw his clothes on the bed, grabbed his pillow with such force that his head bounced off the mattress, threw the covers back and punched him in the arm. Reluctantly, he got up, got dressed and left.

With kids ranging in age from 6 years to 5 months, she was finally through. God help her, part of her still loved him and a bigger part of her hated him and she'd never let him move back in.

THURSDAY, SEPTEMBER 23RD

Garden City Hospital only let fathers and grandparents on the Maternity Floor and since Taylor and Connie weren't pregnant or wearing robes and slippers, a nurse stopped them and asked them who they were.

"I came to see my husband's baby," Taylor said.

"Oh, one of those. The Nursery is down the hall. Honey, just wait a few minutes till shift change and there will be so much confusion nobody will notice you and you can see the baby," the Nurse patted Taylor on the arm and walked away.

"That's got to be her, she looks just like Little Van when he was born" Taylor said. Sure enough, "Valentina Poole" was printed on the card on the end of the clear plastic bassinette.

"Isn't that what you were going to name Little Van if he was a girl?" Connie asked.

"Yep, they stole my name."

CHRISTMAS EVE, DECEMBER 24TH

Evelyn called Taylor and asked her if the kids could come over to her house Christmas Day. Taylor told Evelyn that as long as Sue and her kids weren't there, she would drop them off for a few hours. There was still a little part of her that didn't think it was right to keep the kids from their grandparents. After all, was still on friendly terms with Bob.

CHRISTMAS DAY, DECEMBER 25TH

Thena was divorced and two year old Matt was spending the day at his other grandparents' house with his father. After a bad breakup with Al, Thena decided that marrying a guy that wasn't from Warrendale would work and it didn't. The tragedy of it all was that no matter who they married, Al and Thena still had feelings for each other, they knew it and everybody else knew it too.

Thena and Taylor drove around for a few hours in Thena's 1968 green Dodge Charger with bucket seats and black leather interior, looking at Christmas lights, singing along with Christmas Carols on the radio, bitching about their current unfortunate circumstances and killing time. At 5:00PM, Thena pulled up in front of Evelyn's house.

"That's Van's car and he'd better be alone," Taylor said.

Thena watched Taylor walk up to the house. She looked at the picture window and saw a lot of people but through the shears she couldn't really make out who anybody was. Then she saw Sue's car two doors down on the other side of the street. In a blink of an eye, Taylor was out the door running with her kids back to the car.

Sarah, Vance and Vanessa sat in the back seat and Baby Van was on Taylor's lap.

"She's in there, isn't she?"

"She's in there."

"So, did you kids have a good time?" Thena asked. As much as she wanted to swear and yell, it was still Christmas.

"No," Sarah answered.

"No, why not?"

"There are little girls in my Grandma's house calling my Daddy 'Daddy' and a baby they said is my sister."

"Oh no, they didn't," Thena whispered to Taylor.

"Oh, yes they did. I told Evelyn she traded four for four."

"We don't have our presents," Vance said.

106

"Do you want me to go get their presents?" Thena asked.

"No. We'll go to K-Mart tomorrow and you can each pick out one toy, whatever you want," Taylor said.

"I want a present from Mommy, I don't want anything from them," Sarah said.

"That baby isn't our sister cuz you're not her Mommy. We don't even know her Mommy. I want a doll," Vanessa said.

We shouldn't have to do damage control on Christmas Day; these kids should have one day out of the year where they don't have to deal with their father's bullshit, Thena thought pulling away from the house.

"And a doll you shall have," Taylor said.

"I'm glad Matt is too little to know anything other than presents," Thena said.

Baby Van smiled and grabbed for the gear shift on the console, "Oh no you don't," Thena laughed. He would have no memory of this day, of ever being at his grandparents' house or of Sue and her daughters and that was a good thing.

CHAPTER THIRTEEN

1972
JANUARY

The only thing that changed about Van was his address. He was partying more and working less. Ray heard Massey Ferguson was hiring and convinced Van to go with him to fill out an application.

"What should I put here were it asks for hobbies?" Van asked.

"Put fertility god," Ray laughed.

They both got hired into Massey but by March, Van quit. He didn't like working on the line. It reminded him of the first job he had at GM when he got home from Nam. He didn't' like it there either.

Taylor and the kids had settled down into a routine. She found the perfect babysitter to watch them at night when she was at work., a little old lady the kids called "Grandma" Between Grandma, Big Joe and Lorraine, Taylor was doing better than when Van was around. Lorraine kept telling her Van was nothing but dead weight and she had to admit that Lorraine was right. Money was tight but she wasn't on edge wondering about who Van was screwing or what he would screw up. Sarah was the only one that asked when Daddy was going to come and see them and even she wasn't asking that much any more. She was still mad that he told her she had another sister because she knew who her sister was and it wasn't that baby. Taylor could tell that Vance had an "oh well, it is what it is" personality and Vanessa had a combination of both her nosey and Vance's "oh well" but Sarah worried her because Sarah wouldn't let anything go.

MARCH

Gloria went off for days at a time without coming home or checking in with her mother so Mary didn't think anything of it when she hadn't heard from her daughter. But days turned into three weeks and Mary's new husband reported her as a missing person.

APRIL
A SATURDAY AFTERNOON

Gloria's disappearance was the hot topic of conversation up and down Warren Avenue and Taylor, Thena and Lorraine were no exception.

"I wonder how long before Gloria turns up dead?" Thena asked.

"That's cold," Lorraine replied.

"The truth can be cold."

"I thought she was dating a nice guy and quit screwing around."

"I know him. He is a nice, quiet guy," Taylor said.

"That sure doesn't sound like Gloria's type," Thena said.

"His friends warned him not to go out with her but the heart wants what the heart wants. The cops questioned him, Van and a couple other guys."

"How do you know that?" Lorraine asked, ready to bitch Taylor out for talking to Van.

"The grapevine at work, bar people gossip."

"I hope it was at least an accident and she wasn't murdered," Thena said.

"What's wrong with you? We don't even know she's dead," Lorraine said.

At the same time Thena and Taylor said, "Oh, she's dead."

OCTOBER

A badly decomposed female body was found by a man walking his dog in a field by the Huron River in Ann Arbor. The news reported that some of the bones were missing but the skull was there and her teeth were all in tact. There were remnants of a red and white checkered ruffle blouse, denim jeans and one white tennis shoe.

Thena was watching Channel 7 News and called Taylor, "This may sound crazy, but I think they found Gloria's body."

Taylor was a true crime murder book junkie and read every book she could get her hands on, with stories spanning from the accident scene to reconstruction of the crime to capture of the murderer so she had a lot of knowledge of how the system worked. She knew that if there were any teeth remaining in the skull like the news reported, if the body was Gloria, she'd be identified pretty quickly and she was right. It only took the cops a few days to make a positive ID and they immediately questioned Gloria's boyfriend again. This time he took them out to his car, opened up the trunk and they found the hammer he used to smash in her skull wrapped in a bloody towel covered with dried blood and dyed black hair.

"They say he snapped. She was running around on him, he told her he loved her and asked her not to and he snapped," Taylor said.

"But why didn't he ditch the hammer?" Thena asked.

"Stupidity, because he loved her and he wanted to get caught."

110

The following Saturday night Thena and Taylor went to the First Edition, singing "G L O R I A Gloria" over and over again with the juke box and got drunk. Thena's cousin, Dean, was the bartender so they drank for free. When they told Lorraine what they did, she told them they were warped.

December
First Week

Christmas was three weeks away and Taylor and Thena found the idea totally depressing so they decided to get babysitters and go hang up at The First Edition. Dean was sitting on the other side of the bar getting a buzz on when they walked in.

"Hi cuz, what's shakin?" Dean asked.

"Well, it is almost Christmas and that's depressing and add to that Larry's in town so I guess nothing good," Thena answered, she sat on the bar stool to the left of Dean and Taylor grabbed the one on his right. Larry was their born again relative that never missed an opportunity to be obnoxious or preach to their family that he just couldn't get to see the light. "He told me that the devil doesn't need to go looking for you and me because he already found us."

"No, shit," Dean laughed. "Bartender, set me and the ladies up. Let's not disappoint Larry."

"This seat taken?" Dave Sullivan asked.

"Nope," Thena answered.

"Taylor Ginetti, is that you? I haven't seen you in a long time. Didn't I meet you at Taylor's house?"

"Yes you did and you called me a bitch," Thena answered."

"Ouch," Dean said.

"You did call her a bitch," Taylor interjected.

"You were a bitch," Sullivan continued.

"If that's your pick up line buddy, it won't work," Dean said drinking his beer.

"What do you care?"

"Lay off, he's my cousin."

"He talks too much. You want to go out tomorrow night?"

"Sure, why not."

Dean shook his head, Taylor laughed and Thena figured she was overdue to have some fun.

"What is wrong with you? He called you a bitch," Dean asked.

"Sometimes I am."

"So am I," Taylor added.

"And here I sit between two bitches."

"And don't forget the devil." Thena laughed.

* * *

Thena and Sullivan started dating but he had one glaring flaw, he still hung around with Van.

CHAPTER FOURTEEN

1973

It was the 70's and their waterfalls were replaced by long hair and headbands; they still wore shades, tank tops or t-shirts with cut off jeans and tennis shoes but their straight legged Levi's were now modified bell bottoms. Viet Nam was winding down and most of the guys were finally home but they didn't come home alone, they brought malaria, jungle rot, nightmares and terrible memories they didn't even talk about with each other. Their drug addiction and alcohol intake increased, along with their enthusiasm for felonious pursuits.

Ted stayed in the service longer than the rest of the guys. When his hitch was finally up, Gwen met him at his ship when it docked in San Diego. They spent the weekend together making wild, crazy, passionate love and then she made a big mistake. She gave him an ultimatum, marry me or we are through. He loved her, he really did. He'd loved her since he was 17 years old but get married, no way. He told her the only way he'd ever be up on an altar was in a pine box. Her heart was broken but she refused to lose her pride so she packed her suitcase and flew back home to the guy who proposed to her. The guy she asked to give her time to think. The guy she married.

When Ted got back home, he applied to the Detroit Police Academy and was accepted. He figured after patrolling the dirty rivers and canals of the Mekong Delta, the streets of Detroit would be a cake walk..

After his last tour in Viet Nam, Wayne was stationed at Whitby Island in Washington State. He developed a serious relationship with a girl he met in Seattle and he decided to stay there when he his hitch was up. Out of all the guys, he is the only one that didn't come straight back to Detroit.

* * *

Outside girls came and went, and they always brought a girlfriend or two with them, so along with Liz came Jen and Lisa. Boone knocked up Liz; she was average looking, big boned with brown hair and taller than Boone so, of course, Evelyn didn't like her. Ken Kowalski knocked up and married Jen and Al Kopka and Lisa got drunk one night and eloped.

After a bad break up with Al and a violent marriage that ended in divorce, Thena was living with Dave Sullivan and watched the endless parade of girls come and go. Most of the girls had good paying jobs, the rest were stay at home Moms. Sometimes the guys worked and then they didn't work, but they always partied. The only guys that kept steady jobs were Sullivan, Boone, Kowalski and Buzz. The other guys would pick up jobs as their money was running out, sell dope or commit various crimes and fence their ill gotten gains. One by one they were getting married, having kids and trying to stay straight but they were always drawn back because they were friends by seniority.

They lived within two miles of each other in houses and apartments off of Warren Avenue or in duplexes and apartments on Fitzpatrick Court. Boone and Liz rented the apartment across the hall from Dupree, his girlfriend Joyce and their daughter. Dupree's hustle was selling drugs but his downfall was that he used more than he sold. He never held a legitimate job and Joyce supported him. One of his cons was to get the owner of the apartment building to make him the Manager. Then he proceeded, with the help of a couple of the guys, to remove one pane of the double pane windows from every window in every apartment and sell the glass for drug money.

* * *

They staked out their own section of Hines Park off Warrendale Drive in Dearborn Heights. They had picnic tables, bathrooms and trees for shade. Hines was about 5 miles from their neighborhood and went for 17 miles, running along the Rouge River and ending in Northville. Even though it ran through seven cities and townships, it was like being in the country.

They were in Hines Park during the day and at night they hung out mostly at the Warrendale Bar or Dupree's apartment. Chorty's, Warrendale and Zenia's Bars were next door to each other so from time-to-time they would wander into Chorty's and Zenia's but Tim, not being part of that crowd and an undercover Detroit cop, rarely wandered into the Warrendale or Chorty's, he had his permanent stool at the bar in Zenia's. Now the guys called him Tim the Cop.

The guys that weren't working would show up at Hines in the afternoon with their kids, everybody else would show up early evening after they got off work and bring their kids. To people passing them in the park, they looked like a normal group of people, tossing Frisbees, laughing, talking and challenging other guys in the park to race for money. Sullivan was the fastest so he was their designated runner and he always won. They were hustlers and masterminds in illegal activities. If they would have channeled their energies in honest pursuits and instead of illegal activities, they could have all been millionaires.

Van's good looks were fading. He was down to one girlfriend and an ex-wife. He brought Sue's girls to Hines everyday but she rarely showed up. She was smart enough to stay away.

Sam Smith, a/k/a Buzz, started dating Sue's best friend Alice; they both had custody of their five year old daughters from previous marriages and they actually seemed like a happy, normal couple. His day job was bartender at the Hyatt in Dearborn so he was clean cut unlike the rest of the guys, he had short hair and no mustache or beard. At night sometimes he'd moonlight as the bartender at the Warrendale. Because he had to be so polite during the day, he was more of a smart ass at night. Alice was an assistant in an ear, nose and throat doctor's office. From listening to conversations, Thena could tell that Alice was intelligent. She was approximately the same height and weight as Thena; she wore her black hair in a long shag, like Thena wore her hair, and wore wire rim glasses like Thena. Damn Thena thought, she could be me. For weeks, Alice and Thena stared at each other but didn't talk or sit at the same picnic table. Then one day Alice walked over and sat across from Thena.

"It's kind of like looking in a mirror, isn't it," Alice said.

"It is weird, I'll give you that," Thena replied.

"I know who you are."

"Most people do."

"You're Taylor's best friend."

"And you're Sue's and I'm being polite by using her name. I usually call her something else."

"I've heard, why Rocky Raccoon?"

"With all the black makeup she has circling her eyes she looks like a raccoon, plus she likes living with garbage."

"That's pretty good. Look, she is my friend, but I sure as hell am not his. We have a mutual dislike of each other."

"He seems to be losing his touch. There was a time he could charm any girl."

"I have nothing against Taylor and I don't think we should be enemies because of Van."

"Look, I don't want to fight with you either but I'm telling you straight up I do have something against Rocky."

"I don't like what she's doing but she is still my friend."

"He killed her kids' father. Those kids have to look at him everyday and they know he killed their father. How does somebody do that?"

"I don't know, I really don't know."

"One of the reasons I come to Hines is to keep an eye on Missy, Eileen and Kathleen. The losers here are the kids and we both care about the kids."

"I heard a rumor that Missy wasn't Mark's kid. Is that true?"

"Nobody else claims to be her father. How is that for an answer?"

"I get it. Look, Alice, I like you and under different circumstances, we might even be friends. I can see that."

"There is really no reason for us not to get along."

"We have one thing in common, we both hate Van."

"And think how it will piss him off if we get along."

They raised their Coke bottles in agreement and from that day on when they were at Hines, they sat across from each other. Thena respected Alice for taking the first step because she never would have done it; she could tell that Alice was nobody to mess with and she was glad they were on the same side. She told Taylor about their conversation and Taylor agreed it was a good thing.

* * *

Thena understood why Boone stood up for Van but why he trashed Taylor was a mystery to her. Was it loyalty because she divorced his brother or was it more than that? Had Evelyn brainwashed him into believing that Taylor was the reason for Van's problems? They would argue and agree to disagree but her fights with Van were vicious. She would stare him down with her *"die you son-of-a-bitch"* look and he would give her his *"fuck you bitch"* look. They fought so much that people either stood around and enjoyed the sarcastic remarks they threw at each other or ignored them altogether. Van had a short fuse and Thena knew how to light it. She enjoyed aggravating him and depending on her mood, she would assault him with different levels of insults.

117

One sunny, summer afternoon Van and Thena were sitting across from each other at the picnic table. She had PMS and it was no holds barred. She pointed her right index finger at him (known as the 'Warrendale finger') and said, "No matter how much ink you slap on top of that tattoo, I know that ribbon says 'Taylor'."

Alice burst out laughing and Sam shook his head.

"Sullivan, shut your old lady up," Van yelled.

"His old lady? You ass, I wasn't his 'old lady' when you stole my car and drove to Jayne Fitzgerald's house."

"Again with the car, I didn't steal your damn car. I brought it back. Jesus, how many years ago was that?"

"Thena, when you're right, you don't have to argue."

Every once in a while Dave said something that she thought was profound and this was one of those times. After that day, unless Van approached her and was so drunk and obnoxious she couldn't ignore him, she tried not to argue with him. She wasn't always successful, but she did try. However, through the years they called a truce three times, at Boone's, Ray's and Al's funerals.

* * *

Even though Dave and Van grew up a block away from each other, he didn't like the way Van treated Taylor or their kids. He knew first hand what it was like to come from a broken home and he told Van more than once that he needed to make things right with Taylor because he was acting like a dick but now Van had screwed his life up so much, Dave thought Taylor and the kids were better off without him.

CHAPTER FIFTEEN

1974
MEMORIAL DAY WEEKEND

Thena enjoyed the weekend day trips to Dupree's land on Murphy Lake. Everybody played in the water with their kids, they would water ski, bar-b-que, toss the Frisbee, shoot off fireworks and they actually acted like normal families. On the way home, they would always stop in town and get an ice cream cone. But she hated the weekend campouts because they were a completely different story.

Dupree's land was on the end of a dirt road at the end of the lake and cops never came out that far so it was anything goes. They would drink, smoke, drop whatever chemical anybody had on them, hit the bong and party all night long; there were no kids and it was not a family affair. The guys didn't fight but because a lot of them brought along their broad of the moment, verbal chick fights were not uncommon. The broads of the moment were like alpha dogs that felt the need to piss all over and mark their territory. Thena, Liz, Lisa, Jen and Joyce hung together and would laugh at these broads because the guy they were marking as their own usually had a wife and kids sitting at home. They secretly wondered how often it was their old man with another broad while they were sitting at home.

Thena really hated camping. One night in a tent was more than enough for her and two was way too much. She refused to pee or do anything else in the woods, so if nature called, she drove into town. Even though the rest of the girls laughed at her inability to piss in the woods, one or more of them always rode into town with her.

Thena and Dave were sharing a tent with Al and Lisa. They didn't own a tent because she refused to pay even a little portion of her hard earned money for something she didn't want. Dave really wanted a tent but he had to choose between sharing a tent with somebody else and Thena's wrath; he chose sharing a tent. Dave and Al were wasted and stumbled into the tent around 3:00AM. The tent was pitched on a slant so when Al stepped over Thena to pass out next to Lisa, she was sure he was going to roll down and crush her.

Al and Dave's combined snoring was earsplitting and she couldn't sleep. She even hit Dave in the back a couple times but that didn't work. She couldn't believe that Lisa was sleeping through the noise when she felt like her ears were going to bleed from the assault. She laid there trying to fall back to sleep but it was useless. All those times that she wondered what it would be like to sleep with Al, this wasn't what she had in mind. So after an hour of fighting back the urge to punch them both in the mouth, she grabbed her Levi jacket and stepped outside. She stood next to a tall pine tree and looked at the moon reflecting on the lake. The sky was clear and she could see the stars. Now if I were in a cabin with plumbing, this would be great she thought. Then the sound of a terrible hacking cough penetrated her thoughts and she saw Van sitting alone at the picnic table next to the smoldering camp fire. She walked over to the side of the tent so she could get a better look without him seeing her. All resemblance to his former self was left to photographs and memories. He was an overweight, out of shape, balding man, doubled over, throwing up blood. Everybody knew he had bleeding ulcers but he kept on drinking. Was he drinking to live or drinking to die she wondered. She was mesmerized; standing there in the dark watching him and she was sad because he had thrown his life away. She stood there a little while longer and watched him walk down to the lake and wash the blood off his mouth and hands and then she went back inside the tent. Thena climbed into her sleeping bag and even though the snoring stopped, she still couldn't sleep because now she was haunted by Van and the blood, there was so much blood.

Thena waited to tell Dave what she saw until they got home. He just shook his head and told her there was nothing anybody could do and to forget what she saw. There wasn't much chance of that ever happening.

JUNE

Both Lorraine and Thena's first marriages ended in divorce which shot their theory that they would live happily ever after if they didn't marry a Warrendale guy all to hell. Lorraine had been living with Butch Baranski and Thena had been living with Dave in the same apartment and duplex complex for over a year when they decided to give in and married them. Taylor thought they were nuts but then she hadn't approved of them living with Butch or Dave either so she kept her mouth shut and thought time will tell. After all, it wasn't like she had the best track record to give advice, not that either one of them asked her. They were going to do what they wanted no matter what she said so why piss them off.

JULY

"My case worker said I have to sign a complaint against Van or they will cut off my ADC. He is supposed to pay money to them and he never has. I don't want to do it. I don't want all those people pissed off at me," Taylor said.

"And if you don't do it, you lose your ADC, and he still doesn't pay any money. You don't have a choice," Thena counseled.

Van was arrested and thrown in Wayne County Jail a couple days before the hearing and the Thomas clan was on a rampage. It didn't matter to them that Van didn't support his kids and, of course, they blamed Taylor. If she got a better job she wouldn't need ADC and Van wouldn't be in jail. He had to make a $500.00 payment to ADC to get out of jail and he didn't have the money.

Boone called Dave and it was short conversation.

"I'm going up to Chorty's for a beer," Dave said.

"Don't you dare help throw bail money for him," Thena said.

"I'm not."

"You're lying. I'm watching the kids so she can go to Court and you're helping bail him out? This is fucked up."

CHAPTER SIXTEEN

1975

JANUARY

The guys were starting to move out of Warrendale. Van and Rocky rented a house in Detroit off of Fenkell. Boone, Ray and Dave bought houses in Redford, minutes from each other; all-in-all they moved less than 10 miles from Warrendale Avenue. Their wives hoped those 10 miles would be enough to get their husbands to settle down. They worked steady, played with their kids, mowed their lawns, kept their houses up and their cars running but they still partied at the bars, in Hines Park or they would meet up at Dupree's apartment on Saturday nights to watch the Ghoul and Froggy. It didn't look like that would ever change.

Taylor stayed in the house her Dad bought her. The kids were doing well; she was still working as the part-time bookkeeper at the First Edition and on ADC and as much as she would have liked to leave the neighborhood, she could pay the bills and that was what mattered because she sure as hell couldn't depend on Van for any help and her Dad had already helped her too much. Van still paid the occasional visit and at first Taylor couldn't figure out why but out of sheer nosiness, she tolerated him. Sometimes she thought it was guilt that motivated him, sometimes she thought he just wanted to see what she was doing but the real reason, the reason that she finally settled on was that they couldn't entirely let each other go; and then there were the late night phone calls from Tim when he was in the bag, professing his undying love.

APRIL

Al and Lisa separated shortly after the Memorial Day camping trip the year before. She realized it was time to get clean and sober and try to find the life she would have had before the fatal car crash. While Lisa got on with improving her life, Al's went into a steady decline. His hair was down to his shoulders and he looked like he hadn't shaved since she left. Between drugs and booze, his life was spiraling out of control. He didn't have a job, sold dope to make money and he had no permanent address. Wherever somebody let him stay is where he lived. Wherever he could score and have a good time is where he went. The real Al had disappeared and was replaced by a homeless, jobless drug addict but, of course, none of the guys noticed or cared. The girls noticed; the girls cared and Joyce had a front row seat because she saw him every day at her apartment doing drugs or scoring drugs from Dupree.

A FRIDAY NIGHT

Jim Farmer was a cadet in the Detroit Police Academy and he liked to walk on the wild side. He wandered in and out of Warrendale, not enough to be considered one of the guys, but just enough so they would let him party with them. Thena and Joyce didn't like him, they thought he was just a little too slick. The story isn't clear why Al was at Farmer's party that night. Dupree said he was dealing, others say he was just partying. Whatever he was doing there, it sealed his fate. When Al overdosed, Farmer panicked and instead of calling an ambulance, he dragged Al's body out the side door and through the alley. Two girls at the party followed Farmer and watched him roll Al into the street on the next block. Farmer went back to his party and the girls ran and got their car. By the time they got to Al, he was foaming at the mouth. It took them 20 minutes to drag his convulsing body into the back seat. They dumped him at the ER door of the nearest hospital and took off. They'd lost their buzz and they didn't want to be questioned by the cops. Al's condition was too bad for a small neighborhood hospital to handle so Wayne had him rushed to a bigger hospital. Wayne sat in the ambulance next to his brother, praying that some how some way everything would be okay, not knowing that Al's fever had reached a brain boiling temperature and his kidneys were destroyed.

Wayne's parents put him in charge. He would make all of the decisions. He was no longer easy going, Viet Nam changed that. He would do everything he could to find out what happened. In the days that followed, he tried putting the pieces of each story together but he never got enough information to complete the puzzle. There were too many people with too many stories. But one name kept popping up over and over again in every story, Dupree.

Van and Dave went to the hospital every night. Van always called Taylor after he left the hospital. Thena and Taylor compared what Dave and Van told them so they could get a better handle on the situation. Their reports were so similar they were confident the guys were paying attention to what was going on. The one thing they all knew but were never able to say to each other was there was no walking away from this one, Al was going to die.

FRIDAY, MAY 2ND
4:00 PM

When Dave thought Al's condition was as good as it was going to get, he told Thena she could go to the hospital to see him. Thena was four months pregnant and Dave was worried how she would react when she saw Al tied down with tubes in his sides for dialysis, up his nose and in his arms, but he was more afraid of what she would do if Al died and he didn't let her go to see him. He hadn't told her how Al looked because he was afraid to. Her childhood friend, Dee Dee, said she would take her to the hospital; Dee Dee could handle it, Jill, Ann and Taylor couldn't and Lor flat out wouldn't do it. Dee Dee would take her but she wouldn't go into the room. That she couldn't handle.

A nurse led Thena in the direction of a small, separate room at the end of the ward. She could see two beds through the large window. She saw Al in the bed on the left and another man in the bed next to him with just as many tubes and machines on him. She stood in the open doorway trying to take it all in. Al's eyes were closed, she took a deep breath and walked in.

SATURDAY, MAY 3RD
5:00AM

Thena grabbed the phone on the nightstand in the middle of the first ring.

Van called; Al died at 3:30 this morning. Did you hear me?" Taylor asked. She didn't call Thena sooner because she couldn't quit crying but Thena could tell, she knew, they had been friends too long.

"I heard you."

"Lisa is up north with some guy, Joyce is calling her. Are you okay?"

"No. I'll talk to you later. Bye."

Thena got out of bed and went into the living room. She sat on the couch in the dark with her hands resting on her belly. The phone didn't wake Dave or Matt and she needed this time to herself. Al was dead. How could this happen? How did everything get so fucked up? She didn't blame Lisa for being up north with another guy. Lisa confided in Thena she knew her marriage to Al was a big mistake; then she gave Thena some advice, "Never get married drunk or with a broken heart." Thena just couldn't wrap her head around the fact that they all knew Al was dead before Lisa did. Less than 12 hours ago she was looking into his tear filled eyes and his wrists were tied with strips of cloth, when he opened his hand for her to hold. She held her left hand up in front of her face, she was holding his hand with this hand and now he was gone. She put both hands over her face and sobbed.

8:00AM

The first call Thena made was to Tim. She never dropped a dime on anybody in her life but this was different. He was an undercover narc and she gave him all the information she had. The drugs came from Dupree and everybody thought that Connie's chemist husband, Warren, made them but they couldn't prove it. Tim called Ted, who was a uniform cop, and they took it from there.

The second call she made was to her parents; the third call was to Jill. Jill broke down and they cried together.

NOON

Taylor called to see how she was doing.

"I called the hospital and asked about his condition. They said he wasn't a patient there anymore. I had to check. I had to know what they would say."

"I did the same thing," Thena said.

They couldn't decide if they were searching for the truth or morbidly curious; once again, Lor said they were warped.

WEDNESDAY, MAY 7TH
THE FUNERAL

Taylor and Lor never went to funerals. Unlike Taylor and Lor, Thena always went, either out of duty or out of respect, she couldn't figure out which but today it was because of love; a modern day Romeo and Juliet tragic kind of love that Al left her behind to survive. The funeral home was packed with family, neighbors and friends and she tried not to breakdown and she kept telling herself if she did, there were so many people there that nobody would notice. She looked around the room at all the flowers and plants, she dreaded walking up to the casket. When the tears started to roll down her cheeks, they didn't stop. She stood there, looking down into the casket. The beard and long hair he had five days ago were shaved and cut away and the man lying in the casket looked like the boy she knew so many years ago. Silent tears were joined with uncontrollable sobs. Dave grabbed her by the shoulders and walked her out of the room, into the hallway and shoved her back against the wall.

"Look at me, get a grip. I'm not playing around," he ordered.

"I know. It was just a shock to see him like that. He looked like he used to," she sobbed.

"His mother had them do it. She didn't like the way he looked. It's what his mother wanted."

"Sullivan, give her a break. She's pregnant and this isn't easy for any of us," Van said.

"Why is she crying like that?" Liz asked Lisa. They were standing together in the back of the room with a clear view of the hallway.

"They were engaged once," Lisa answered.

"Well she sure kept that secret."

"It's no secret. People from the old days know. He still has her graduation picture. It's a nice picture, an 8 x 10 oil in

128

a leather folder. He saved it from when he was in the Navy. I'm sure she still has stuff from him too. I know how she feels, just not for him. I made the mistake and married him, she didn't and that's why she still loves him."

"She still loves him! Gee, I wonder how Sullivan feels about that."

"Liz, let it go. Let her mourn him. I still mourn Steve and I probably always will. That's how I got myself into this fucking mess, trying to deny it. So here I stand, a widow that doesn't grieve for her husband but instead for another man and there she is grieving for him and married to somebody else."

Rumor was Wayne was packing a Dirty Harry, a .44 Magnum. He stood guard next to his brother's casket and waited for Dupree but Dupree never showed; he must not have been feeling lucky.

At the wake Tim and Ted told Thena the Jim Farmer situation was handled. He was kicked out of the police academy and he had disappeared. It had been suggested to him that he leave town if he didn't want to assume room temperature. Thena never told Dave that she was feeding information to Tim because he would have quit telling her what he knew. Even though Tim was one of their own, in Dave's eyes he was Tim the cop.

JULY

Dupree's drug habit increased to the point it became too much for Joyce and she took their four year old daughter and baby boy and moved out. The guys cut him loose, the only one that talked to him was Sullivan and that was only if Dupree called him.

NOVEMBER

Thena was sitting in the overstuffed chair feeding Maria her bottle. When she looked up from the TV, she was surprised to see Van and Boone standing on her front porch. She thought maybe they came over to see her new baby girl but that was so not like them.

"Come on in. I'll be right back," Dave said leaving her, Matt and Maria alone in the living room with them.

"Okay, you're making me nervous standing in front of me like that, sit down on the couch until he gets back from whatever he's doing."

"She looks like Sullivan," Van said.

"She does not," Thena said. "You just said that to piss me off."

"She sort of does," Boone chimed in.

"Both of you shut up, she looks like me."

"I don't know, I think she looks like me," Dave said walking upstairs from the basement and handing Van one of his rifles.

"What's going on?" Thena asked.

"Opening day rifle is tomorrow," Van said.

"I know that. Dave, what in the hell is going on?"

"Time to go guys," Dave said.

"Where is Van going with your rifle?

"Hunting."

"You just gave convicted felon your rifle. Hello, felons can't have guns."

"Relax, he's just going hunting."

"Whatever happens, it's on you. The kids and me won't be dragged into it."

"Kowalski and me are meeting them in Stockbridge tomorrow morning."

"Oh even better, when he gets caught you'll be there and get hauled in too!"

"You worry too much."

"Really, well one of us has to."

CHAPTER SEVENTEEN

Thena was in the middle of loading the dishwasher when the kitchen phone rang. She answered it on the second ring and was balancing the receiver between her shoulder and ear as she dropped the silverware into its designated spot.

"Hello."

"Get Sullivan," Boone ordered.

"Dave, its Boone; something's wrong."

"Son of a bitch. Okay, take it easy and we'll be right there." Dave said.

"Take what easy and we'll be right where? Thena asked rolling the dishwasher over to the sink and pulling out the hose to hook it up to the kitchen faucet.

"Van tried to kill himself."

"The doctor was right. This is number two."

"What are you talking about?"

"When he overdosed on the Vicodin the doctor told Taylor he would try three times and on the third try he would succeed."

131

"You never told me that."

"I didn't know you didn't know. It isn't exactly something that comes up in a conversation."

"Liz is at work with their car so I've got to take him to Van's and I said you would watch his kids. Grab the kids and let's go."

"Matt, honey, come on," she said throwing diapers and wipes into the diaper bag.

"Ernie," Maria said.

"Babycakes, you really don't need a knit hat. It's not cold out."

"Don't argue with her, just put the damn hat on her head," Dave said hotfooting it out to the car.

Thena put Maria's Ernie hat on her head, tied it under her chin and grabbed the diaper bag.

"Where are we going Mommy?" Matt asked.

"We're going to Brandon's house."

Dave was in the driveway with the car running. Thena put Matt in the backseat of her 1973 Charger and held Maria on her lap.

"Tried to kill himself how?" Thena asked Dave.

"He stuck his head in the oven."

"He called from the oven?"

"Don't laugh Athena, it isn't funny."

"I think it's funny. Is it an electric oven?"

"Get it all out of your system now."

Boone was standing in his front yard when they pulled up.

"What took you so long? You're only five blocks away."

"Sorry, my fault," Thena answered, helping Matt out of the car. She knew it hadn't even been 10 minutes since he called but it must have seemed like forever to Boone.

"The kids are watching TV," Boone said and they were gone.

Matt ran in the front door and sat on the floor in front of the TV with 5 year old Brandon and Baby Cassie. Thena sat Maria on the floor with the other the kids and persuaded her to let her take off her Ernie hat. She stood in the kitchen doorway so she could keep an eye on the kids and called Taylor. This was too good a scoop not to immediately share.

"You are not going to believe this," Thena said.

"Try me," Taylor replied.

"Well, Boone called Dave because Van put his head in the oven and said he was going to kill himself."

"Wait a minute, he put his head in the oven and called Boone to say he was going to kill himself with his head in the oven?"

"Yep and Boone told Dave he called the fire department because the gas was on and they would meet the firemen over there."

"Did anybody put an apple in his mouth?"

"I don't believe you just said that but I love the way your mind works. The only place that pig is going to roast is in hell."

"God's going to get us for laughing."

"God has to have a sense of humor don't you think? At least I hope God has a sense of humor or we are both going to be sweet talking St. Peter. I'll call you when I get home."

As soon as she hung up the phone it rang and she thought it was Taylor calling back.

"Hey, oh, hi Evelyn. Nope, he's not here. Why am I here? I'm watching the kids. Why am I watching the kids? Boone went out with Dave and Liz is at work. *Don't laugh, don't laugh* she thought. Well, Evelyn, Dave drove him to Van's house because Van stuck his head in the oven but I am pretty sure he is okay because he called from the oven. No, Evelyn, I haven't told anybody. Yes, they are over there now. I don't know if the phone is still working. If I hear from them, tell them you are on your way. Got it, bye."

Thena went into the living room and sat down to watch TV with the kids. She hoped Dave and Boone would get back before Liz got home but she wasn't that lucky.

"What's going on? Where's Boone?" Liz demanded.

Hello to you too, Thena thought.

Thena retold the story being very careful not to laugh, smile or even snicker. Liz had a big mouth and Thena knew if she made any type of sarcastic remark, it would come back and bite her in the ass. Liz was married to Boone and they were friends by acquaintance, nothing more.

"Wait just a minute. I want to make sure I've got this right. You're telling me that he called from the oven?" she said picking a sleeping Cassie up off of the floor.

"Yep, and Evelyn doesn't want anybody to know."

"He's an asshole. Between Van and Evelyn, I don't know how Boone isn't fucked up. Now she's ordering me to keep my mouth shut to protect her precious son. I am so telling everybody."

"That's between you and Evelyn."

"Mama, home," a sleepy Maria said crawling up into the chair and onto Thena's lap.

"Soon, sweetie." It was almost 9:30PM and Thena's patience was running thin with the entire situation. She had two tired kids and had to deal with Liz and Evelyn in the same day. She was not amused.

At 9:30PM Boone walked in the front door.

"Thanks for watching the kids. Dave's in the car," he said.

"So did you pull your idiot brother's head out of the oven?" Liz asked.

"Not now, Liz," Boone said.

"Come on Matt," Thena picked up Maria and the diaper bag and walked to the car.

"What took you so long? I had to deal with Evelyn and Liz."

"Van's really fucked up."

"He's been fucked up for years."

"This is different."

"Oh, spare me."

"He's got nothing. His kids don't even know who he is and Rocky left him."

"So she finally left him? Well, he brought this on himself and I don't feel sorry for him. He's not my problem and he's not your problem and don't make him our problem."

"Damn it, Athena, can we not do this now. I know he did this to himself but he's my friend and there's nothing I can do about that."

"He's left a lot of bodies in his wake. And as for Rocky, she got just exactly what she deserved. As far as I'm concerned they both killed Mark Poole."

"That was a long time ago."

"I know exactly how long ago it was."

"Let it go."

"Let it go, is that what you said? Let it go? Tell that to Mark Poole. Oh wait, you can't because he is still reaching for the door."

"Athena, I said I don't want to fight. It's been a rough night."

"Maybe, just maybe, now those little girls can have a normal life. As much of a normal life as they can with that bitch for their mother."

* * *

A month after what the crowd dubbed "the 911", Thena saw Alice at Hines.

"How are Rocky's kids?"

"They seem to be doing well but I look in their eyes and it's like there is a lot going on in there but they know not to say anything. Sue has created this alternate reality for them. It's like Van never existed. She torched all the pictures of him and she told the girls that Mark died in a car accident."

"But they saw Van shoot him."

"I know but she doesn't think they remember."

"It would be a blessing if they really don't remember but too many people know the truth."

"It is like she is in a self imposed Witness Protection Program. She's changed her name and other than her family, I'm the only one that knows where she is. Even if the girls remember anything, they won't talk to her about it. She doesn't know Kathleen remembers because she told me her Daddy was in heaven and Van sent him there. I'm not telling her because I don't want her to twist Kathleen's mind any more than she already has."

"Damn."

"And as far as Valentina is concerned, Sue is going to let her believe that Mark was her father too."

"Taylor's kids know Van is out there somewhere but other than Sarah asking where he lives every once in a while, they don't act like they really care. He wasn't really around the younger ones that much. But they all know Van killed a man. Taylor tried to hide it from them but little pitchers have big ears and then there is the outside world. I think it is better that they know the truth. They didn't believe Evelyn when she told them Valentina was their sister so it's not like they are ever going to look her up."

"We are talking about eight kids here, that are all going to grow up and become adults some day. One of them is going to want to figure things out."

Alice was right and that one kid, after she got married and had a couple kids of her own, was Valentina.

CHAPTER EIGHTEEN

1977

TAYLOR

Taylor figured her life was as good as it was going get. She would always have to struggle to survive and knew she could never trust a man again but her whole family was healthy, her kids were doing well in school, Big Joe was dating a nice widow named Grace and Lorraine was still married and seemed like she was happy. Her bills were getting paid, there was food on the table and most of all, other than her kids fighting with each other, there was no drama in her life. Thena told her what was going on with Van but she could hear his name, listen to what he was doing and not get upset. She considered that quite an accomplishment and one she never thought she would achieve. She still hadn't forgiven him but at least she had gotten herself to the point where she thought if she had to ever deal with him face-to-face, she could.

She was tending bar two afternoons a week for the lunch crowd and that's where she met Danny. He was from the neighborhood but he never hung around with Van and the guys. She had seen him around and knew who he was but they never really talked. He was good looking with dark hair and brown eyes, he was close to 6 feet tall, with a good build and a sweet smile. He sat down at the bar, took of his black leather jacket and threw it on the empty stool next to him, sitting there in his black t-shirt and jeans, she liked what she saw.

"I'll have a cheeseburger medium with everything, fries and a PBR," he said.

"Fried onions?" she asked opening the bottle and setting it on the bar in front of him.

"Please."

"American or Swiss?"

"American."

"Coming right up."

"Stay and talk to me," he said lifting the long neck to his lips.

"Well, that's kind of hard to do since I have to throw your burger on the grill."

"I'll move down to the end of the bar. I bet you can talk and cook at the same time."

"Since this is the end of the lunch hour rush, and you are the only customer right now, I think I might be able to pull that off."

She didn't know he had taken a late lunch because he wanted to be the only one in the bar. He wanted her undivided attention and so far his plan was working.

"I've been wanting to talk to you for a while," her back was to him but he could see her reflection in the mirror behind the bar.

She smiled, flipped his burger and turned around, "Is that so, about anything in particular?"

"How about a date?"

"You move pretty fast. No, I don't think so. I don't date Warrendale guys. They don't make good dates or anything else good for that matter."

"Ouch. That's an unfair generalization don't you think?"

138

He uses words with more than one syllable, Taylor thought. This might be promising.

"So you expect me to believe you've got a steady job, you're not a drunk and you're not a bum."

"Oh, now I am wounded," he said slapping his right hand over his heart. "I'm a chemist at Ford. I pay my bills. I enjoy beer but a bum, no. I'm not a bum."

"I have four kids."

"I know. I don't scare easy either. I've never been married, no kids, I'm not a bum, no jealous ex-girlfriends out there. Now what more could you want?"

"What kind of car do you drive?"

"A Shelby."

Taylor laughed. "This is your lucky day Mr. 'I'm not a bum' because I love Mustangs. You've got a date."

* * *

Taylor had another part time job two days a week with a delivery service. She delivered important documents to attorneys' offices, filed pleadings with Courts and she was especially busy during tax season making deliveries to CPAs. She could get a run as far away as Port Huron or as close as downtown Detroit. She never knew where the next delivery was going to take her; she was seeing different people all the time and other than superficial pleasantries, she really didn't have to interact with anybody. She loved the freedom.

One steamy summer afternoon she had just completed her last delivery of the day and was heading home. The light turned green and she accelerated when an old Chrysler Newport came barreling through the intersection, slammed into the driver's side fender of her Lincoln and kept going until it hit a telephone pole. She sat there for a minute, collecting her thoughts, checking out various parts of her body making sure nothing was broken. She moved her neck from side-to-side once or twice trying to determine if she had whiplash before she got out of the car to continue her assessment of the situation. She was on Schaefer and not too terribly familiar with the area but familiar enough to know she was not in the best part of town.

She walked over to the Chrysler to see if the driver was injured because she didn't see any movement over there. The front end of the Newport was totaled with the front bumper and hood wrapped around the telephone pole. There were three teenage guys in the car, two in the front and one in the backseat. It didn't take a part time bartender to figure out they were all drunk.

"I don't suppose there is any use asking you for your driver's license and registration?"

"Give me a minute, man," was the slurred reply.

God looks after babies and drunks, she thought. Minnie told her that during one of their many kitchen chats. There wasn't any blood, they didn't act hurt and they weren't going anywhere any time soon so she walked back to her car. A crowd was beginning to gather over by the telephone pole but so far nobody had approached her, thank God. Her car was facing the wrong way, her fender was smashed and her headlight broken. Her tire wasn't flat and her rim wasn't bent so she figured she should be able to drive it home. Lucky she wasn't in a smaller car or the impact from the Chrysler would have been a lot worse.

She stood alongside her car still trying to clear her head, when a guy came up behind her and said, "Hey Mama, what's shakin'?"

"What's shakin'?" she whirled around to confront the familiar voice and there he was in all his glory with a red dew rag tied around his head, hair down to his shoulders, a dirty white tank top and jeans ripped at the knees. Now she knew she was in shock because she was looking at Tim, undercover narc detective Tim, and she just stared at him, amazed as he strutted by and gave her a wink. He had called her a couple nights before professing his eternal, undying love and begging her to run away with him to which she replied "sober up". This was the first time she's seen him on

140

the job and she was fascinated with his undercover persona but not enough to run away with him.

A few minutes later Ted's squad car pulled up.

"We got a call about an accident situation," Ted smiled. "Want to tell me what happened maam?"

"Why yes officer, I would love to."

VAN
AUGUST

Most of the guys were living with girls or married and were starting to settle down. They still played on the bar pool league but more and more they were becoming weekend warriors and spending more weeknights at home with their families.

Everybody liked hanging around at Boone's house on Saturday night. He had four lots of land beginning on a corner surrounded by trees. His house sat on the front of the corner lot and the rest was vacant land. The early part of the evening the kids would play on the swing set, throw baseballs or Frisbees and color at the picnic table but when it started getting dark, home they went to babysitters while their parents came back with lawn chairs to sit around a campfire to drink and chill. Van would either show up with some strung out bimbo in a halter top and short shorts or alone stoned out of his mind.

The wives and girlfriends sat at one end of the campfire so they could trash talk without their old men telling them to zip it.

"Where does he pick up them up? He's always got a different one?" Amy asked

"He gets them high so they think he looks good," Thena said taking a sip of her rum and coke.

"There's not enough stuff to get me that high," Liz chimed in.

"I told him whatever flavor of the week he has, I don't want him bringing them over to my house and I mean it," Jen said.

"Flavor of the week, I like that," Thena laughed.

"He still thinks he's God's gift," Dana added to the conversation.

Thena flashed back to him washing the blood off in the lake.

"I don't think that's it. I just think it's all he knows how to do," Thena said.

"You're the only one that knew him when. Was he ever any good?" Dana asked.

"You know, so much has happened with him and Taylor and the kids, I don't think I can be objective any more. I think I liked him when I was 12. I think I liked him until he came home from Nam. But then he tried killing himself and when he took my car that did it."

Dave walked up, pulled Thena out of her chair, sat down and placed her on his lap.

"He took your car, let me guess your talking about Van," he laughed.

"Sullivan, what brings you over to our end?" Amy asked.

"I just wanted a chance to talk to you lovely ladies. And you do look lovely tonight."

They all laughed because they knew he was blowing smoke.

"Oh my God, what do you want?" Thena asked.

"You ladies don't believe me. I can tell these things. I'm really hurt you would think I had a motive for wanting to sit with you. I just started to think that we are acting like we are at a dance where the guys stay on one side of the room and the girls on the other and I want to surround myself with your beauty."

"And he said all that with a straight face. This must be big."

He lit his cigarette, took a long drag and kissed Thena on the cheek.

"Now sweetheart, there might be one favor I'm looking for."

"He wants a blow job in the car while he's driving," Amy laughed.

"No, he wants a three way," Dana laughed.

"Ladies, get your minds out of the gutter. While that all sounds pretty damn good, that's not it. Thena, Boone and Van are going to camp out here with Brandon, Vance and Little Van next weekend and they want to know if I want to bring Matt. What do you think?"

"Wait a minute, Van with Vance and Little Van? I think there is more to it than you are telling me, that's what I think."

"Amen, sister," Amy said.

"He called Taylor and she said it would be okay," he continued.

"Dave Sullivan, this is the first I've heard of it," Thena said.

"This is the first I've heard of it too," Liz said.

"Well he just now went into the house and called her," Dave said.

"Would you just spit it out because I know there is something you aren't telling me."

"Come on Sullivan, spit it out," Dana laughed.

"Christ, I can't talk to all of you at once. Look, Vance and Little Van said the only way they would come with Van is if Matt and me are there."

"Bingo. Why didn't you just say that in the first place?"

"Maybe because I didn't think the whole world should know, okay."

"I think it's funny. So let me see, I hold the power right here in the palm of my dainty little hand. I will decide if I want Matt to camp out next Saturday night. It might be too chilly, he might catch a cold. I don't know. I just don't know. What will I ever do? It is such a big decision for little me."

143

"Enjoy yourself, I'm going back to the friendly part of town," he said pushing her off his lap. He knew how much she hated Van but he also knew she would call Taylor tomorrow and that is when the decision would be made.

SUNDAY

"So what's going on with this camping deal?" Thena asked Taylor.

"Van called last night and asked me if he could take the boys next Saturday night to camp out at Boone's."

"And you said?"

"My first instinct was to say fuck you, you haven't seen them in how long and now out of the blue you want to play Daddy but I didn't. I told him to let me ask them and call me back in ten minutes. So I talked to them, they said they didn't want to go and I thought maybe it wouldn't be such a bad thing so I told them I thought they should go and they said the only way they would go is if Matt and Dave went and that sounded like a good idea to me. The funny thing is the only one that wants to go is Sarah and Van told her it was boys only."

"So now it all makes sense. Okay, I'll tell Matt he's going camping. Tell Vance and Little Van that Dave and Matt are going."

"And you will let me know how it goes."

"I always do."

SATURDAY

Van knocked on the screen door but Vance and Little Vance opened up the door and ran into the living room. They'd never had to knock on Matt's door, they always went right inside. Van walked inside and stood in front of the door.

Thena was sitting on the couch and Vance sat down beside her.

"We don't want to do this. We don't know anybody. I don't know why he wants us to be with him. He never has before," Vance said loud enough for Van to hear him.

"I'm not going to tell you that he is a good Dad because he's not. But I am going to say if he wants to spend some time with you and you can have fun doing it, why not?"

"Is he really our Daddy?" Little Van asked sitting next to Vance.

"Yes, he's our Dad. You've got the same name, don't you?" Vance answered.

"I hate my name. I want to go home."

"Everybody hates their name," Thena said.

"They do? Do you hate your name?"

"I do."

"Does my Mom hate her name?"

"You can ask her that when you get home but let's talk about what is going on now. Okay?"

"Okay."

"I'm not going to make you go but I really do think you will have fun if you do. It's a nice sunny day, it will be a good night to sleep in a tent. You know Dave and Matt, that's two people. You'll see your Uncle Boone and his son Brandon is your cousin. If you decide you aren't having fun and you want to leave, Dave will bring you right back here or home, wherever you want to go. If you just want to talk to your Mom, Liz is there, she is your Uncle Boone's wife and she will let you call your Mom. I already talked to her about it."

"That's a promise," Dave said walking into the living room.

Matt came running out from his bedroom dragging his sleeping bag on the floor behind him.

"Why don't you boys go out on the front porch? Your Dads will be out in a minute," Thena said, kissing them all on the cheek.

They looked so much alike wearing their Tiger baseball caps with their fair skin, blonde hair and blue eyes Matt could have been their brother.

"You're coming, right Dave?" Little Van asked.

"I'll be there in a minute."

"If they want to come home, you better not give them a hard time," Thena told Van.

"He's not going to give them a hard time," Dave said.

Van just stood there staring at Thena.

"You look pathetic. If you weren't such an asshole, I would feel sorry for you."

"I know I'm an asshole but thanks for reminding me."

"Your welcome." She watched Little Van take Dave by the hand, walk down the porch steps and then they were gone.

"Hey Taylor, it's me. They just left. I think they'll be just fine."

CHAPTER NINETEEN

Taylor decided to let Danny move in with her and the kids. She was doing exactly what she didn't approve of Lorraine and Thena doing but they did it and God didn't strike them dead so she thought what the hell. She hadn't changed her opinion about trusting a man and if she ever found out Danny cheated on her, no matter how much she loved him, he was gone. In her mind it was a practical arrangement with emotional benefits. He would help her pay the bills and keep an eye on the kids. The kids liked him, especially Vanessa and Little Van. She was having some trouble with Sarah who was showing symptoms of the same type of manic depression that Van was diagnosed with years before. Vance had a bad ass angry streak. He would do anything for his Mom and sisters; he would knock Little Van around every once in a while just to keep him in line but nobody else had better ever lay a hand on his little brother. Danny and Vance had an understanding, as long as Vance came home at a decent time and Danny didn't give his mother any grief, they were golden. Danny knew they had a very low opinion of their father and he wanted them all to know he was there for them if they needed him, but he didn't want to be their father. Because of their grandfather and Uncle Carlos, they knew there were good men in the world and Danny figured that is why they were willing to cut him a break. Van was living in Marlette with a broad named Marti that had two little girls. Danny was glad that Van left town because he really didn't want to get into it with him but if he had to, he would. It disgusted him that Van would hook up with chicks that had kids and play Daddy but he never came to see about his own. They were a family now and as far as they were concerned, Van was in the past.

Taylor went to night school and got her GED. She wanted to start taking night courses at Wayne County Community College in business administration so instead of doing the books at night at the First Edition, she switched her schedule to doing them in the morning before the bar opened. She never had a scarlet letter sewn on her shirt but all these years she felt like she had one stamped on her heart and now she was starting to feel like she could actually improve her circumstances and quit feeling like the bad, frightened, knocked up little girl that she had been carrying around inside of her all these years. She had to admit that hooking up with Danny had a lot to do with that, Danny and the fact that Big Joe was always there for her. He took care of the maintenance on her cars and seeing that the yard work was done before Vance was big enough to start doing it. If he hadn't bought her the house, she didn't know where they would have ended up living. Every day she thanked God for her father, Aunt Chi Chi and Uncle Carlos because she knew she never would have made it without their help. And she never forgot about her Grandma, may her soul and all the souls of the faithfully departed through the mercy of God, rest in peace. Amen.

JUNE

Taylor saw Van standing on her front porch but she ignored him and kept watching TV. He had lost more hair but at least he was keeping what he had shaved down. He was wearing clean jeans with a tie died tank top and he actually looked presentable. He still had a beer gut but the definition was coming back in his arms. She wanted to see how long it would take for him to knock on the screen door.

"Taylor," he finally called out and she ignored him. Damn it, she thought, he was going to knock on her door like the stranger he was.

"Taylor, I know you can hear me. Taylor, I can see you," he called out again pounding on the door. Her hair was long again. She got it cut short, just below her ears after Little Van was born. He liked it better long. She was wearing black rimmed glasses, shorts and a t-shirt and he felt a jump in his heart. The kind of jump he felt as a kid when he looked at her. The kind he didn't know he was still capable of feeling. He wasn't as dead inside as he thought. For a split second he was standing on her parents' front porch on a Saturday afternoon with Tim watching her walk to the door to let them in.

Pounding or knocking, it was the same thing, it required permission to enter.

"Taylor, can I come in?"

"The kids aren't here," she replied.

"I didn't come to see the kids, I came to talk to you."

"Gee, that's a surprise. You can come in but don't plan on staying long."

"I just need a couple minutes," he said and sat down on the opposite end of the couch.

She was watching *Sergeant York* starring Gary Cooper. The last time she watched it was years ago with Lor, Thena and Tim and every once in a while when they were goofing around they would mockingly say "Alvin" like Joan Leslie's character Gracie Williams said to Gary Cooper's Alvin York. She loved the otherwise sappy movie for that reason.

"Didn't you hear me calling you?"

"I heard you."

"Then why didn't you answer me?"

"Friends call out to friends, strangers knock."

"We aren't strangers damn it. You know you, Lor and Thena are the most sarcastic, evil tongued women I have ever had the misfortune to come up against."

"That's quite surprising considering all the women you've been up against, and I mean that in the most literal sense. But I think I am going to take that remark as a compliment and on behalf of my sister, Thena and myself, I accept the award for sarcasm." She stood up and bowed on her way to the fridge for a cold Pepsi. "I'd offer you one but you won't be here long enough to finish it."

She sat back down on the couch and looked him in the eye, "Enough bullshit, why are you here?"

"Did you know that my brother has lung cancer?"

" I heard."

"He is going to marry Cathy so she can get money when he dies."

"That's as good a reason as any to get married I guess."

"You should have told me when your Mom died."

"Don't bring my mother into this, that's ancient history," Taylor said putting her cigarette out in the ashtray sitting on the middle couch cushion.

"We really should quit smoking," he said lighting a Camel.

"There is no we".

"I heard Dan Zilenski lives here."

"You heard right. The kids like having him here in case you were wondering like the concerned father you are."

"I don't want to fight, Taylor. I just wanted to let you know that I love you and you are the only one I will ever marry."

"Is that supposed to make me feel good because I really could care less if you get married and we've been over and over the love thing. We have been out of each others' lives for a long time."

"But not out of each others' blood."

"Don't speak for me."

"You know we had something special."

"We had something special, you and Jayne had something special, you and Maureen had something special, you and Rocky had something special and named her Valentina. What's your point?"

"Some day you are going to have to forgive me."

"Oh, I forgave you a long time ago but I will never forget. There is a difference."

"Please, just remember what I told you."

"I remember everything you tell me. I remember every single lie you've ever told me."

"Maybe some day you will like me again." He kissed her on the forehead and left.

She wondered if the reason for his visit was because he found out Danny lived there. He could have been coming off a bad hit of acid or having one of his manic moments she really didn't care. She didn't care, but she wondered what he was up to. Sooner or later, she would figure it out.

AUGUST

"Remember that little visit Van paid you a while back?" Thena asked.

"It's burned into my memory. Why?" Taylor asked.

"Well, this weekend, it seems the whole Thomas family and the Warrendale crew are on their way to Marlette for a wedding. A wedding I might add that Dave and I are not invited to. Can you imagine how upset I am to miss the wedding of the year, maybe even the century? Marti's daughters are going to be flower girls, isn't that precious. And the wedding is outside in a field."

"Well, you really can't afford a hall on unemployment checks and welfare." So much for him never getting married again. Just another one of his lies."

"But what was the point? I don't get it."

"That's his brain on drugs. But I would be lying if I said I didn't wonder what his little visit was all about. I wonder if Evelyn approves of this daughter-in-law.

"Word is she isn't too happy about Boone's new wife."

"If my son was dying and married a hootchie mama like Cathy, I wouldn't be happy either."

"This chick is way past hootchie mama, she may be married to Boone but she's fucking Kowalski. Even if Boone did marry her so she could get his life insurance, she should show him respect while he is still alive."

"If you ask me, they all deserve what they get. I don't wish cancer on anybody but Boone hasn't said one word to me since the day Van killed Mark Poole. Does he see his kids? Does he support his kids?"

"Since the divorce, he hasn't seen them that I know of. As far as supporting them, according to Liz when I run into her in the grocery store or at the kids' school, she's not getting any money from him either."

"So Boone's getting fucked over, join the club."

"But don't you think it's tacky of Kowalski. I mean his friend is dying and he's fucking his wife."

"I didn't say I didn't think Kowalski was an ass and how he lives with himself, who knows. Gee, does his perfect little ex-wife know what he's up to?"

"Jen moved out to Howell by her parents. I don't think she has anything to do with him anymore and he's another one that doesn't see his kid or pay child support."

CHAPTER TWENTY

1979
TAYLOR

Taylor was happy, she was actually happy. Her best laid plans were working out. Danny asked her to marry him and she said yes. They hadn't set a date yet but she had a beautiful diamond ring, one she wouldn't have to take a ride to Michigan Avenue to pawn. She lost count of how many times she asked Thena to drive her to the Pawn Shop and sit in the car with the kids while she pawned her wedding rings or got them out of hock when she was married to Van.

Thena and Dave had their third kid, a baby boy in February. They named him Michael. Two weeks later, Lor and Butch had their first baby, also a boy. They named him Anthony.

Yes, life was looking up for everybody.

VAN

Van came to Detroit a lot, always alone. He would stay with one of the guys that didn't have an old lady that objected to his flopping there. His honey never came to town with him and he wanted to keep it that way. He was so used to leading a double life, he wasn't willing to give it up. Sometimes he called Taylor when he was in town to tell her how Boone was doing but he never talked about what was going on with him or ask what was going on with her. She wondered if he called Rocky too, he didn't. She had let the kids spend a week with him and his wife in the summer. They said it was okay but they didn't want to do it again. At least this time there wasn't a baby he told them was their sister.

NEW YEARS EVE

Taylor sat at a table at the First Edition with Danny, Dave, Thena, Lor and Butch, listening to the band, watching people dance, holding confetti in her hand and waiting for the stroke of midnight to throw it in the air and yell Happy New Year. They were decked out in their finest clothes. The girls were wearing long dresses and heels and the guys were in suits and ties.

"You're smiling," Thena laughed.

"I am?" Taylor replied. "I'm happy. It's been a good year."

"Yes it has, we've come a long way," Lor said.

"Here's to us," Danny said.

"To us," Dave said.

They lifted their bottles and glasses in a toast, clinked them together and yelled, "Happy New Year."

CHAPTER TWENTY-ONE

1980
FEBRUARY

It was pool league night at the Warrendale, every stool at the bar was occupied, the tables were full and the bar was hopping. A few Grandale girls were sitting at a table watching the match between their old men, Kowalski and Sullivan. Buzz was busy tending bar when the phone rang.

"Warrendale," he said. He had taken so many of these calls over the last couple years that when he heard Dana Hammond's voice he knew in his gut it was bad news.

"Dana, I'm sorry. I'll tell them. If I can do anything, let me know." He hung up the phone, poured himself a shot of Jack Daniels straight up, sat on his stool at the end of the bar and downed it.

"What's going on?" Boone asked.

"Ray's dead. He came home from work, laid down on the couch and died. She couldn't find anybody's phone number so she called up here."

The pool game stopped. Kowalski and Dave propped their cue sticks up against the wall and looked at each other like *what the fuck?* The Grandale guys zipped their cue sticks up in their cases, grabbed their women, said they would catch them later and headed to the Blue Star Bar to get drunk. They knew Ray and even though he wasn't one of their own, he was way too young to die. They, along with Warrendale, were feeling all too mortal.

"What the hell happened?" Dave asked.

"They don't know. The Wayne County Coroner's got him."

"I was over his house yesterday. I couldn't' find a damn clamp for Thena's Charger radiator hose and he made one for me."

"When is this going to end?" Van shouted.

"It's not," Boone whispered.

"Jarzembowski or Sajewski?" Kowalski asked.

Every funeral of every guy was at these two funeral homes, two blocks apart from each other on Warren Avenue.

"Step," Buzz said pouring himself another shot.

"Maybe that's a good sign. Maybe changing funeral homes will stop the curse," Mike said.

"He's at Step because it's in Redford," Dave said.

"You guys really believe there is a curse?" Van asked irritation rising in his voice.

"I do think we are cursed. I don't know why we are cursed. But hell yes, I think we are cursed," Mike said.

Some of the girls blamed all the dying on Van because they believed that ever since he murdered Mark Poole the whole neighborhood was cursed. The wives and girlfriends worried more with each death and the guys increased their drug and alcohol intake. The wives and girlfriends got more responsible while the guys got more reckless. It was a vicious circle with no end in sight.

Van lifted his beer bottle in a salute to the juke box and sang "I'm on the Highway to Hell and I'm going down all the way down" along with AC/DC.

"I'm outta here," Butch put on his black leather jacket, grabbed his car keys, cigarettes and Zippo off the bar and left.

156

Dave punched the Temptations *Papa Was a Rolling Stone* into the juke box and they were quiet. There just wasn't anything else to say.

* * *

Thena didn't want to go to the funeral home. She wanted to remember the good times like Ray sitting on the curb with her in front of Taylor's house talking and gossiping. There was one conversation that stood out from the others, the day Ray told her he knocked up Dana and they were getting married.

"You know me. I've already got two kids and I never got married but I love her."

"I think that's a good thing. I'm happy for both of you."

"You know my sister and me are adopted, right?"

"Yep."

"My parents are great and everything but I don't want my kids to wonder who their Dad was like I wonder sometimes. I mean, like was he big like me, you know? You know who your parents are. You know who you look like."

"I do."

"I know I'm not the best Dad. Hell, I'm probably not even a good one but my kids know who I am. Hell, if I thought their mothers weren't taking care of them I would step up but I know they have good mothers and good homes."

"That's a cop out. Don't look at me like that, you know I speak the truth."

"If you were a guy I'd deck you," he laughed.

He could be a mean mother fucker when he was wasted but when he was sober he was like a great big teddy bear. She wanted to remember the good things. She wanted to remember his smile and his laugh. She didn't want to remember him in a box.

* * *

The funeral home was packed. Butch, Dave, Van, Boone and Mike were standing in a small circle in the hallway between the two viewing rooms, looking down at the floor

157

and then Van looked up and asked the question that was weighing heavily on all of their minds, "Who's next?"

They looked up at each other, from one face to another. How many had died since 1971? They could name every name and how they died from drugs, suicide, motorcycle accident, gut shot by a jealous husband, car accident and until Ray, all were violent deaths. Yes, they could name them all and the way they died but they could not, they would not count them because they were afraid they were getting to the point where there were more of them dead than alive.

Thena stood by herself, behind Dave, listening to the guys talk and it scared her. She looked to her right into the room where Ray's body was but she never left the hallway. She watched Ray and Dana's daughter, Ramona, standing on the kneeler, staring down at her Daddy and it broke her heart. Ramona had long blonde hair and was big for her age like Ray's two older kids. She heard Ramona say to somebody, "Daddy's in heaven but he can see me." A jumble of thoughts kept running through Thena's head. She couldn't remember how old Ramona was. She thought she was around 5 or 6. It was important for Ramona to remember her Daddy. It was important to know how old a little girl was when she lost her Daddy forever. She didn't know why that was important to her but it was. All the guys standing in that circle were fathers. Some of them better fathers than others. If Van died, it wouldn't change his kids' lives at all. If her husband died, one year old Michael wouldn't remember who he was. She knew that Dana was a strong, intelligent woman and she would survive but damn she lived through years of hell with Ray, he gets clean and sober for one year and dies. Where is the justice in that? Ray was even reading the Bible. What was God thinking?

* * *

It took 6 weeks for the autopsy results. Ray had a congenital heart defect and that coupled with a bad case of the flu killed him. Oh, and his insides were like that of an 80

year old man they said as a result of many years of drug and
alcohol abuse. He got straight too late

CHAPTER TWENTY-TWO

1981

JUNE

It was Saturday afternoon and Dave and Thena left their kids with her parents and rode their Chopper downtown. She was wearing her Captain America helmet, the same kind of helmet that Peter Fonda wore in *Easy Rider*. She loved that helmet. Dave wanted her to buy a boring black helmet like his, but she declined. They were wearing tanks tops, jeans and boots. It was beautiful day, the sun was shining, it wasn't sweltering hot out, it was just right.

Every weekend during the summer there was an ethnic festival or some other kind of festival; something was always going on at Hart Plaza. It was a 20 minute ride down to the foot of Woodward Avenue and Thena was enjoying the ride. She wasn't one of those chicks that held onto to their old man for dear life. She leaned her back against the sissy bar, rested her hands on her thighs and feet on the pegs and enjoyed the ride. She sat a bike like she was born to ride. They parked the bike in Ford Garage and walked up the steps to Jefferson Avenue.

Hart Plaza, the structure itself was a gigantic twisted spire of concrete and not much to look at but out in the open, on the lower level was the amphitheater, stage and the rising metal structure in the middle of the fountain with water flowing from the halo looking circle on top. It was on the river front with a great view of Canada on the other side.

"What a great day," Thena said, standing on the top level and looking out onto the Detroit River then she heard it, "KEE AW KEE."

"KEE AW KEE." There it was again.

This cannot be happening, Thena thought. She looked down on the lower level and sure enough there they were standing by the fountain, Van, Mike, Kowalski and some guy she didn't know wearing a Harley bandana on his head.

"KEE AW KEE," Dave yelled back.

"Enough or Jeff and Porky are going to come running with Lassie," Thena said.

They walked downstairs and Thena was horrified when she realized that the guy in the Harley bandana was Boone. She kept trying not to think about the obvious, she tried to smile at Boone and not let the horror she was feeling register on her face. Cancer and chemo ravaged his body and robbed him of every recognizable, unique feature including the gleam in his eyes and his hair. He was unusually quiet. He spoke once and his voice was soft and low. She knew she was looking into the face of death and it made her shudder.

AUGUST

Four funerals in one year was four too many and the year wasn't even over yet. Kowalski was conspicuous by his absence but the grieving widow was front and center.

"Don't start anything," Dave told Thena.

"I'm not going to start anything. This isn't my fight," Thena said.

161

She stood in the back of the room and Dave walked up to the casket alone. At least this time she walked into the room she told herself. She took off her glasses and put them in her purse so she couldn't see the casket. Then her nosiness got the better of her and she put them back on so she could look at Van. He looked lost and alone standing at the foot of the casket. Dave slapped him on the back and stood next to him. She actually felt sorry for him. He looked at her and they nodded to each other. Vita and the rest of his sisters were sitting next to each other in chairs in the front of the casket with Evelyn and Bob. Just like all the other funerals, there were so many flowers.

Boone had moved back into his parents' house shortly after they'd seen him at Hart Plaza and Evelyn took care of him until he died. Thena wondered how many people in the room knew that Kowalski moved into Boone's house and was fucking his wife.

"I use to see you at parties, now its funerals." Amy said.

"I know, it sucks," Thena said.

"Did you see the gold ribbon on the spray of red roses on the casket?"

"No, I can't walk up there. The last casket I walked up to was Al's. I won't walk up to any more."

"It says Loving Husband."

"You've got to be kidding."

"At least at Al's funeral Lisa had class enough not to pretend the situation was anything other than what it was. I'm glad Kowalski had brains enough to stay away."

"So you know?"

"Oh yeah."

"Does anybody else know?"

"I would venture to guess, pretty much everybody. I don't see that many people talking to her, do you?"

"This is the first time everybody knew and nobody said anything."

"Well, it's really beyond sick don't you think? As soon as Boone moved home, Kowalski moved in but I guess these guys will never stop passing around women. How is Taylor?"

"She's good."

"Does she know?"

"Van called and told her. She won't be here."

"Liz just walked it. She's looks pissed."

"Thena, why didn't you tell me Boone had cancer?" Liz demanded.

"Shouldn't you pay your respects before you start bitching me out?" Thena shot back.

"I was here before, I already paid my respects but only Vita and Van would talk to me.

"The Thomas family doesn't like exes, just ask Taylor. How was I supposed to know that you didn't know?"

"Well, I didn't or I wouldn't have taken him to Court for child support. That's why all these people hate me."

"Don't take this out on me. You think I'm the only one in this room that knew he had cancer? And if you think that is why his family doesn't like you, you are delusional."

"What do you mean by that?"

"Oh, please. Evelyn doesn't like anybody her sons hook up with and she especially never liked you and you never liked her and you are trying to pin this on me? I don't think so."

"She's right, Liz. Let it go. Look, I'm going home and heat up some soup and check on my kids. Why don't you come home with me, have some soup and we can talk?" Amy said.

Thena, tell Mike I'll be back will you?"

"I'll tell him."

"What was that all about?" Dave asked.

"How was I supposed to know she didn't know Boone had cancer? What was I supposed to do give her a call and say by the way, Boone has cancer? She is a friend by acquaintance and the reason for the acquaintance is gone. Our kids see each other at school and that's it."

"Let it go. Lets get out of here, I can't take it any more."

"First, I've got to tell Mike Amy went home but she's coming back."

There wasn't an empty space in Sajewski's parking lot and people were still flooding into the funeral home. They climbed in the back of their custom Ford Van with the smoked windows and changed into cutoffs and tank tops and headed for Hines. They sat at a picnic table by themselves, smoking, drinking a pop and talking about everybody that died. Ray and Boone were the only natural deaths, if you could use death and natural in the same sentence.

"This isn't normal, everybody dropping dead," Dave said.

"Do you think there is a curse?" Thena asked.

"Don't ever say 'curse' in front of Van."

"Van's not here."

"This is between you and me and I don't want you even telling Taylor what I'm going to say. Sometimes I wonder if they told the truth about what happened. Maybe if they told the truth and Van did some time, real time for what he did, then maybe just maybe all this wouldn't be happening. It's like guilt by association. I don't think anybody believes they told the truth and so far two of them have taken what really happened to their graves. It's like they made a deal with the devil."

"And the devil is the lie?"

"The devil is the lie."

"Taylor said that since the day the cops picked them up at her house, not one of them has talked about it. Amy said Mike pretends like it never happened and I know Boone never talked about it to Liz or she would have said something. As chatty as Ray was, he never ever mentioned that day to me."

"Van got a telegram today, delivered right to the funeral home."

"Oh my God. What did this one say?"

"The old I'm waiting stuff but they added the wrong brother died."

164

"What did Van do?"

"He was real calm when he read it then he handed it to me to read. When I gave it back, he folded it and put it in his shirt pocket.

"Sometimes I think the Grim Reaper is hanging around wherever we go, with his black hood and cape, just waiting for his chance to drop his scythe."

"Jesus, Thena, you re giving me the creeps."

* * *

Matt saw Brandon at the Detroit News Paper Station a couple days after Boone's funeral.

"Mom, I told him I was sorry his Dad died and he said 'what for, you knew him better that I did'. Mom, I didn't know what to say."

"Honey, you did the right thing, there was nothing more to say."

NOVEMBER

Thena and Dave were watching TV when the phone rang.

"It's after 10:00PM," Dave said.

"I bet Taylor and Danny are back.

Hello, Taylor."

"How did you know it was me? Never mind. Van's dead," Taylor said. "We just got back from Niagara Falls. I was only gone three days. What the hell? This is crazy, I never go anywhere."

"I know," Thena replied.

"She took my kids."

"Who took your kids?"

"Vita, she left a note pinned to a lampshade in my living room. Van's dead, she took the kids and sent Grandma home. I called Grandma and she feels bad because she couldn't stop Vita from taking the kids. What the hell, they found him dead in the woods?"

"Yesterday. The funeral is tomorrow. What else did the note say?"

"That she would bring them home after the funeral. How the hell did he die? She didn't tell me how he died. I figured a heart attack but it wasn't a heart attack was it?"

"Nope, he was shot. They say he shot himself but Dave thinks the Pooles finally got him. I mean his shoulder was blown off."

"I should go get my kids but I can't go there. Everybody knows I don't do funerals. I haven't gone to a funeral since my Grandma died in 1969. The note didn't say for me to go there. They don't want me there anyway."

"We aren't going to the funeral, Dave can't get off of work and I don't have anybody to stay with the kids. I don't think they expect you to go and I think it's better if you don't go. I feel sorry for Bob and Evelyn, both sons die the same year. What are the chances of that? Sometimes grief makes people nicer and sometimes it makes them meaner. It's a long way to go and walk into who knows what. You need to get it together before the kids get home. Even though they didn't know Van anymore, being swooped up and hauled away like that by Vita is going to have some effect on them."

"All the times I wished he was dead, I didn't mean it. Well, at the time I did mean it but now that he's dead, I didn't mean it. I should have never laughed when he stuck his head in the oven or said anything about stuffing an apple in his mouth."

"He was a pig and it was funny at the time. Hey, I wasn't exactly his biggest fan. I probably had more fights with him than you did in the last few years but it is what it is. I do believe he always loved you in his own way."

"We got along great until our feet hit the floor."

"I know." Taylor had told her that many times.

"I think the rifle that he was shot with could be Dave's," Thena whispered.

"What? What are you going to do?"

"Well, nothing right now. Just wait and see what happens. That's all we can do. The only ones that know he borrowed the rifle are Boone, Van, Dave and me and they can't talk and we sure as hell aren't."

"Maybe it was one of Boone's rifles."

"All I know is Dave never got his rifle back. I told him not to give it to Van and I told him to get it back but God forbid he should listen to me.

Make yourself a cup of tea, sit down with Danny and try to watch TV. There is nothing you can do until the kids get back home. I don't even have a phone number for you to call." Thena hung up the phone and sat down on the couch next to Dave.

"How is she?" Dave asked.

"Not good; she feels guilty."

"She doesn't have anything to feel guilty about. He's the one that fucked up their lives, not her. Just because he's dead, doesn't make him a saint. I'll miss him. I've known him since we were 5. Van, Al and me started running away together when we were 13."

"I remember."

"I'm alive and they're dead."

Thena thought about Van asking that ominous question at Ray's funeral earlier that year and now Van and Boone were both dead.

* * *

Taylor was standing on the front porch when Vita pulled up and the kids got out of her car.

"Vita, you crossed way over the line," Taylor yelled.

"Not now," Vita yelled back and pealed away from the curb.

Taylor opened up the screen door and they walked into the living room and threw their backpacks on the floor.

"We're sorry, Mom. We didn't want to go with her, she made us," Sarah said.

"You don't have anything to be sorry for. He is, was your father," Taylor said.

"He was a sperm donor. Don't make it into something it's not. We didn't even know him and he was always living with somebody else's kids. Come on Little Van," Vance said grabbing their back packs and going downstairs to their room.

"Do we still call him Little Van? I mean, Big Van is dead. Isn't he the only Van now?" Vanessa asked.

"You have a point but we can figure that out later," Taylor said.

"I'm tired. I'm going to bed?" Then Vanessa did something she had never done before, she walked over to the chair Danny was sitting in and hugged him.

"Mom, it was awful. He wasn't even in a casket. He was lying on top of a table and he was wrapped up in a blanket and I could see his shoulder was just pushed back on his body. It wasn't sewed on or nothing," Sarah said.

"Did your sister and brothers look that close?" Taylor asked.

"No, they didn't walk up there but I just had to look."

"Believe me, I understand."

"Sarah, you are a brave girl," Danny said.

"The thing is I know I should feel bad but I don't. I feel cheated. I feel like because he couldn't get it together, now I have to deal with the fact that I feel guilty because I don't feel bad."

"Your mother felt guilty when she heard about your Dad dying too."

"You did, Mom, you really did?"

"Sure I did. I thought terrible things about him and I wanted unspeakable things to happen to him and then when he died, well, I felt guilty.

"But she doesn't feel guilty now, do you?" Danny interjected.

"No, I don't because I was thinking irrationally and reacting to his death. I can feel bad that he died but I don't have any reason to feel guilty and neither do you. His life is what he made of it and he chose to not be a part of your lives.

Sarah, he didn't care about himself. Viet Nam, whatever demons he had when he went there, he came home with more but he never talked about it and it just doesn't matter anymore."

"I am the only one that remembers living with him."

"Yes, you are."

"Mom, is it my fault you married him?"

"What are you talking about?"

"You were pregnant with me."

Taylor couldn't believe what was coming out of her kids' mouths but she shouldn't have been surprised because they were, after all, her kids and that meant their minds didn't work in the "normal" way a kid's mind should work. However, she knew that this day would eventually come and had been rehearsing her speech over and over again for years. She put her arm around Sarah and began.

"I didn't marry him because I was pregnant with you; you were a month old when we got married. I was young and my Mom was dead and I did what Grandpa told me to do. I could have said 'no' but I didn't."

"But did you love him?"

"Yes, I did but some how I never really thought it was forever and when you were little, you loved him too."

"Well, I don't now and neither do they."

"And that's okay. He didn't do much to make you or your sister or brothers love him. I want you to know that you kids don't ever have to go with Vita or any of them ever again and I will be talking to Vita. You did the right thing by going with her, you didn't have a choice but that will never happen again."

Sarah hugged her Mom and Danny and went to her room.

"They will be okay. They are tough like their mother," Danny said.

"I hope you're right. I guess only time will tell. Should I call the bitch now or wait until tomorrow morning."

"Tomorrow morning is soon enough."

* * *

"Vita, I'll make this quick. You better never come into my house and take my kids again. You better never go anywhere and take my kids. Do you understand me because I will call the cops."

"Their father died. They are Van's kids too."

"Oh please, do you have any idea how traumatized they are? Do you even get it? Little Van doesn't even remember him and Sarah saw his shoulder was blown off. She knew he shouldn't be lying on a table wrapped in a blanket. What the hell is going on?"

"He was wrapped, covered with a quilt."

"Blanket, quilt, I don't care. These are my kids. Never have any of you, including Van, cared if they had food to eat or clothes to wear. Lor buys them clothes. Have you ever bought them anything or called to talk to them. No. So don't get righteous on me now."

"Would you listen to me Taylor? You have to hear this. When we got there, the funeral director wanted to talk to my Mom and Dad because when it came down to signing papers for the funeral, Marti said she really wasn't legally his wife and she couldn't sign the papers because she didn't want to be responsible for the bill."

"What are you talking about? They had a big wedding in a field with flower girls. Weren't you were there?"

"Well, it was just at a reason for a party because the ceremony was a fake. They hired some guy they met at a bar to play the preacher. There is no marriage license because she couldn't afford to lose her ADC. She told us that when we got there. They just wanted to have a big party. Then my Mom took over and said he was going to be cremated and she was taking his ashes home and putting him next to Boone under her sewing machine. She made arrangements to have him shipped to Flint to be cremated. That is the closest place, Flint. Can you believe that? She figured instead of paying money for a casket, she was paying to have him shipped to Flint."

"So he was just plopped on top of a table."

"Yes."

"Vita, I meant what I said. Don't ever take my kids again."

Taylor called Thena, "Well I guess he was telling me the truth when he said he would never marry anybody but me. That is the only promise he ever made to me that he kept."

* * *

Even though Marti wasn't legally married to Van, she tried to collect Social Security for her two daughters.

"What a greedy bitch. ADC isn't enough for her?" Thena said.

"You know I wouldn't care what the bitch did if it didn't screw it up for me and the kids but now I have to provide all four birth certificates, my Marriage License and divorce papers plus I have to sign an Affidavit all because that stupid funeral guy put her name as his wife on his Death Certificate. Sarah's birth certificate is sealed so I have to go to Lansing to get another copy because I don't know where I put it."

"How in the hell can something like that happen."

"This is proof that it can."

Taylor submitted all of the required documents and it took six months before the checks started to come. Marti still never backed down; she wanted that money for her daughters. Taylor swore that if she ever saw that bitch again, only one of them would walk away and it wouldn't be Marti.

* * *

Van and Boone's ashes were in separate boxes underneath Evelyn's sewing machine.

In 1995 when Evelyn died, Vita called Vance and asked him if he wanted Van's ashes. He picked them up and took the box to Taylor. She placed it in a spare dresser drawer in her attic. A year later she got an unexpected call from Marti,

171

drunk and slurring her words, asking if she could visit Van's ashes. Taylor declined.

ABOUT THE AUTHOR

Athena Morningstar Kelly is the author's pen name.
Ms. Kelly is a Legal Assistant by day and a writer at night
with the dream of becoming a fulltime writer. The single
mother of three and grandmother of four, she enjoys
spending time with her dog, family and friends. She
considers herself fortunate to still hang out with her friends
from the 48227 and 48228.